MOSSBACK '83

C.G MOSLEY

RAVEN TALE PUBLISHING

Copyright © 2025 by C.G Mosley

Published by Raven Tale

All rights reserved.

This book may not be duplicated in any way without the express written consent of the publisher, except in the form of brief excerpts or quotations for the purposes of review.

The information contained herein is for the personal use of the reader and may not be incorporated in any commercial programs or other books, databases, or any kind of software without written consent of the publisher or author. Making copies of this book or any portion of it, for any purpose is a violation of United States copyright laws.

This is a work of fiction. Names, characters, places, and incidents either are the product of the author imagination or are used fictitiously. Any resemblance to actual persons, living or dead, events, or locales is entirely coincidental.

ISBN: 9798309091300

Contents

Chapter One	1
Chapter Two	17
Chapter Three	27
Chapter Four	35
Chapter Five	45
Chapter Six	53
Chapter Seven	60
Chapter Eight	70
Chapter Nine	75
Chapter Ten	80
Chapter Eleven	90
Chapter Twelve	100
Chapter Thirteen	106
Chapter Fourteen	112
Chapter Fifteen	117
Chapter Sixteen	122
Chapter Seventeen	128
Chapter Eighteen	133

Chapter Nineteen	137
Chapter Twenty	146
Chapter Twenty-One	154
Chapter Twenty-Two	161
About the Author	165

Chapter One

Camp Beaver Brook
Tuesday, July 22, 1958

If Chuck Lancaster never saw a baked bean again for the rest of his life, he'd have been just fine with that. He was now in his sixth summer as a counselor for Camp Beaver Brook and this year, as had been the case every year before, baked beans were almost a daily meal offered to young campers. Aside from the unfortunate side effect of flatulence that ran rampant among children who ate the beans, the taste of the legume had run its course with Chuck at least two summers before. As it was now, the mere sight and smell of them made him nauseated.

As he stirred the beans in a deep pot over a flaming gas stove, he reminded himself that this would most certainly be his last summer as a camp counselor. He was on the verge of turning twenty-seven years old and was almost done with college. There was a bright future ahead of him, a future that would never require him to babysit a bunch of smelly, whiny, and bratty children ever again if he so wished. The rest of his working days would hopefully be spent with the animals he'd been studying and training to care for. His father was a veterinarian and so was Chuck's grandfather. Even though it was in his blood, he still had to work hard for his dreams to become a reality. The hard work had finally paid off. Chuck was set to begin working alongside his father in the fall.

"Lancaster! How much longer on those beans?"

Chuck stared into the bubbling pot and felt anger beginning to well up in him. Jake Simpson had been a camp counselor one year longer than him. For some reason, he seemed to think this gave him the right to boss Chuck around. Unlike him, Jake had done little with his time to prepare for the real world as an adult. It seemed he'd changed jobs at least five times since he'd known him.

"A few more minutes," Chuck grumbled.

"Well hurry it up," Jake snapped. "The kids are all in the dining hall. They're hungry and we're gonna have a riot on our hands if you don't grab another gear."

Chuck sighed and reluctantly turned to face Jake. It wasn't just the beans that he'd grown tired of. "They'll get the food when it's ready. I told you it'll be a few more minutes."

Kevin marched closer to him and narrowed his eyes. "If you'd started cooking on time, we wouldn't have to wait a few more minutes now, would we?" His tone was threatening.

Chuck stared right back at him. Jake was one of those guys that loved to run his mouth but did little to back it up. A lot of bark and no bite.

"You know, I'm the senior camp counselor around here," Jake said, jutting out his chin as he spoke. He made the proclamation sound as if he were on the same level as President Eisenhower.

"Yes, and you remind me of that almost daily," Chuck quipped.

"Well maybe I need to remind you of what happened the last time someone got smart with me."

Chuck swallowed and felt his jaw drop slightly. "I can't believe you just said that," he muttered in disbelief.

"Can't believe he said what?" a female voice called out from behind them.

Chuck looked past Jake and spotted Sara Jones standing in the doorway, her arms crossed. Sara was short, petite, blonde, and a real looker. Every other male camp counselor appreciated how well she filled out her Camp Beaver Brook t-shirt. Chuck had been crushing on her since the first day he'd first laid eyes on her. She was one of the reasons he kept coming back to Camp Beaver Brook.

He huffed and shook his head. "It doesn't matter," he said and turned back to the pot of beans.

"Yeah, it definitely matters," Sara persisted. Now she was standing beside the both of them, but her piercing blue eyes were fixed on Jake. "What did you say?"

Jake flashed a smug smile. "Lancaster was getting an attitude with me," he said. "I was just trying to get him to cool it."

Sara's expression twisted slightly. Her brow furrowed. Chuck glanced over and noticed her subtly reach for a large knife that was lying on the counter. She smiled back at Jake, but her grin wasn't smug. Chuck thought it looked maniacal.

"That's all you said?" she asked, slowly moving the knife to her side.

Jake's smile began to fade away. "Yeah," he said. "What the hell is wrong with you?"

Chuck could see that Sara had her jaw clenched, her red lips pursed. She seemed extremely angry.

"I'll tell you what's wrong with me," she snapped. "I've heard from two other counselors that you've been running your mouth again about Joe."

Jake's smile was now completely gone at the mere mention of Joe. He took a deep breath, shook his head, and gave her a bewildered look that, in Chuck's opinion, was completely phony. "Naw," he muttered in his typical southern drawl. "Naw, I ain't said nothing about Joe."

Chuck had now turned his full attention to the confrontation unfolding in front of him. He could see tears beginning to well up in Sara's eyes.

"You think you're so slick, don't you?" she asked, pointing the tip of the knife blade at him.

Jake was now watching the knife and if there had been any hint of arrogance about him left, it had now vanished completely. "W-what are you talking about?" he stammered.

Chuck looked around for another counselor but there was no one else in the kitchen but them. Things were escalating and he was beginning to feel the weight of the burden pressing down on his shoulders.

"You know damn well what I'm talking about," Sara hissed.

Jake smiled nervously and glanced over at Chuck as if he were waiting for him to intervene.

"Sara," Chuck said softly. "Be careful with that knife."

She glared over at him and for a moment he thought she was someone else entirely. Tears were now streaming down her face, but the expression on her face was born from rage, not sadness.

"You're telling me to be careful?" she asked.

She genuinely sounded hurt by his comment which in turn made him feel a pang of guilt. He knew why she was angry, and he knew why she was hurting.

"Joe didn't have to die, Chuck," she said. She was looking at him, but the knife was still pointed at Jake. "He only died because of this piece of sh–"

"No, it wasn't me!" Jake shouted, cutting her off. "Everything that happened was between Joe and Kevin. You know that!"

Sara's full attention now returned to Jake. "I know that last summer you gloated about what happened and now you're doing it again. You have absolutely no remorse for what happened, and someone needs to make you pay!"

"It wasn't me, Sara!" Jake repeated.

For the first time, Chuck felt a hint of sympathy for Jake. What he was saying was true. It was Kevin Parker that had picked the fight with Joe Folsom two years ago. It was Kevin that had pushed Joe, causing him to trip and hit his head on the rock that ultimately killed him. He had admitted to doing it.

"Sara, he's right," Chuck said. "He wasn't the one that killed Joe."

"No, but he could've stopped it," Sara snapped. "He was there."

"We don't know that," Chuck said. "Kevin said he and Joe were alone when it happened."

She waved the knife at Jake. The kitchen lights shimmered off the mirrored surface of the blade. "That's a lie! It's a lie and it's time to come clean!"

"Shut your mouth," Jake said. His brashness was short lived as he raised his hands submissively when Sara waved the knife again.

"Sara put the knife down!" Chuck shouted.

"Not until he comes clean. Tell us where you hid the body!"

Chuck felt his heart pounding in his chest and wished he was now out in the dining hall serving nasty baked beans to the children.

"I don't know where Joe's body is," Jake said. He suddenly sounded more offended than scared.

Sara shook her head, closed her eyes, and began to sob. Chuck quickly moved to where she was, gently took the knife from her hand, and then held her against his chest. She cried and would've probably fallen to the floor had he not been there to hold her up.

Jake stared at them for a moment. He was wide-eyed and still trying to get his breathing back to normal rhythm. Finally, he sneered at Sara and grabbed the pot of baked beans.

"Lancaster, get your floozy under control before someone else has to," he said as he briskly exited the kitchen and into the dining hall.

Chuck wanted to say something back to him. Something that would've hopefully started a fight. In the moment, he wanted nothing more than a good excuse to knock Jake's block off.

"Get me out of here," Sara said suddenly. "I need some air."

"Of course," he said, gently leading her toward the exit.

He opened the back door of the kitchen, and they were met by three more camp counselors: Julie Davis, Earl Holly, and James Dearing.

"Oh my gosh. Is she okay?" Julie asked when she saw Sara's tear-stained face.

Chuck nodded. "She's fine," he answered. "She just needs some air and a break from Jake."

Julie nodded and Earl and James shook their heads.

"We all could use a break from Jake," Earl said.

Julie moved closer, looking Sara in the eyes. "Sara, are you okay, honey? Do we need to call Sally to come pick you up?"

Sally Howard was the camp program director and had taken leave for the night.

"No, please," she said. "I just need to get away for a little while. Can you handle—"

"We'll get the kids fed and to bed," Julie said. "Don't worry, just take whatever time you need to get your head right. Okay?"

Chuck noticed that she stared at Sara for another beat as if there was some personal message being delivered between them.

Sara finally nodded in reply. "I'll be fine in the morning."

Julie exchanged glances with both James and Earl. Eventually she looked over at Chuck. "Take care of my friend, please."

He nodded. "Don't worry about her. Thanks for handling the kids tonight."

By the time they got to the edge of Beaver Brook Lake, the sun had completely disappeared beyond the trees. A bright neon moon began to emerge in the eastern sky and soon the entire body of water was bathed in moonlight.

"I'm so sorry that I lost it back there," Sara said.

They were seated at the end of the pier, legs dangling just above the water. She was leaning against him and his arm was around her.

"It's fine," Chuck replied. "Jake Simpson has that effect on people."

She pushed back from him so she could look him in the eyes. "Chuck, can I trust you?"

He smiled and felt himself blush. "Of course you can trust me," he said. "I care about you."

He winced as soon as the words left his lips. A little too direct, he thought.

"Good," she said, placing a hand on his thigh. "I need to tell you something. I need to get something off my chest."

He licked his lips and gave her a reassuring smile. "Well go ahead," he said. "You can tell me anything."

She gave him a hard look. It seemed as if she were mulling over her decision and having second thoughts.

"Really," he urged. "It's fine. Tell me."

She took a deep breath and nodded. "Okay, but there will be a lot of people mad at me if you blab about this."

Now he was getting really intrigued. "Sara, you can trust me."

Her gaze left him and seemed to move toward the silver moon that was now fully above the tree line. The water in the lake glimmered brightly in the moon beams.

"I was there when Joe died," she said.

Chuck felt his jaw drop open slightly. "You were there?"

She nodded. "So were Julie, James, and Earl. We were all there and saw it happen."

Chuck was flabbergasted and momentarily speechless. He thought back to the day that Joe had died. He'd gotten food poisoning and had been stuck in a cabin the entire day throwing up every thirty minutes. He'd only realized something bad had happened when an ambulance and police cars showed up suddenly.

"You're telling me that you and everyone else have been keeping this from me for two years now?" he asked.

She nodded, and he could see tears again streaming down her face. "It's killing me. I've been holding on to this because I've been told to keep quiet, but it's killing me, Chuck."

He shook his head and felt a tornado of emotions swirling around inside him. "I don't understand," he muttered. "Why was this kept quiet? What really happened that day?"

"That's what I want to tell you, "She replied, glancing over at him. "I want to tell you what really happened."

Chuck looked around in all directions to make sure no one was within ear shot. On the hill behind them he could see the dining hall and all the kids eating inside.

"I'm all ears," he said.

Sara took a deep breath and then opened her mouth to speak. "It started with a dare; a stupid dare," she said. "Joe dared Kevin to climb a large tree on the back side of the lake. He wanted him to climb the tree, walk out onto a branch, and backflip into the water."

This sounded very much like something Joe would do, Chuck thought. The kid was always thinking up crazy stunts that he himself could do, but everyone else would be afraid to try.

"You know Joe," Sara said, seemingly reading his thoughts. "He was always doing that stuff."

Chuck nodded.

"Anyway, as you can probably guess, Kevin refused," she continued. "Joe of course got a good laugh–actually we all did, and then he immediately climbed the tree and performed the backflip."

"I can imagine how much Kevin loved that," Chuck said sarcastically. "It probably embarrassed him."

Sara's eyes widened slightly. "Oh, it did," she said seriously. "It made him mad and as soon as Joe got back on shore, Kevin was pushing him and challenging him to a fight."

"And all of you were still there?"

"Yes," she answered. "We were all there and all of us were encouraging Joe to fight him." She paused and Chuck could see a frown form on her face as she choked back tears. "He didn't want to do it," she said sadly. "It probably could've ended right there had it not been for Jake sneaking up behind Joe and pushing him toward Kevin. Kevin pushed him back and for a moment both he and Jake took turns pushing him back and forth. We just watched it happen. None of us stepped in to stop it."

"And I guess it was somewhere around this time that Joe was knocked to the ground?" Chuck asked.

Sara nodded. "Kevin finally just punched him hard in the stomach. Joe of course doubled over and when he did, he fell to the ground. The top of his head landed on top of a pretty jagged rock. He was hurt badly, and I knew it was a serious situation." She paused again and began to sob.

"It's okay," Chuck said, pulling her toward him. "I can guess what happened after that."

"That's not all," she said, desperately trying to pull herself together. "We of course ran back to the camp to find a phone and call for help. Kevin and Jake stayed with Joe. By the time the sheriff and the ambulance arrived, the two of them had come back to camp too and said that it was too late, that Joe had died. Kevin seemed pretty upset about it, but I always thought it was an act."

Chuck knew a lot of what happened next because by the time help had arrived, he too had stumbled out of the cabin to see what was going on. From what he'd heard, Joe was hurt during a fight with Kevin and that his injured body was still in the woods. What made things more interesting was the fact that Kevin's father was the sheriff of Duke County. What Sara said about Kevin being upset was true, he remembered how frantic he was when he told his father what had happened. However, the series of events that followed had always seemed strange and unbelievable to him.

"So, from what I remember, Kevin's dad and the paramedics went into the woods to find Joe and his body was nowhere to be found," Chuck said. "Unless there is more that you know that you're not telling me."

Sara sighed. "That's pretty much it," she said. "His body could not be found, and they blamed it on a black bear that had been seen in the area."

"I remember," Chuck replied. "A bear randomly showing up and dragging the body away always seemed like a very flimsy explanation to me."

"That's because it is," Sara agreed. "When was the last time you saw a black bear around here? What I think happened is that Kevin and Jake finished Joe off after we all went for help and then pushed him into the lake to hide the body."

Chuck's eyes widened with genuine surprise. "You think they killed him?" he asked.

She nodded. "Yes, I do," she replied bluntly. "Kevin's dad made us all go into the dining hall and basically told us all that it was an accident and that if anyone tried to make it out to be anything else it could spell trouble for all of us, not just Kevin."

"Sounds like he threatened you."

Sara nodded. "I thought the same thing. Julie has always hated it too, but we all made a pact to keep quiet about it. I've just been overwhelmed with guilt because I should've stepped in and tried to stop it. I shouldn't have encouraged Joe to get into a fight with that idiot."

"Well, you're apparently not the only one that felt bad about it," Chuck replied. "Have you heard about Kevin?"

She nodded again. "From what I hear he's pretty much lost his mind. He's stopped talking or socializing with anyone."

"I think he snapped," Chuck said. "I heard Jake say they were going to put him in an asylum. As bad as he was, at least he seems to be riddled with guilt about what happened. Jake on the other hand..."

"Is a complete jerk," Sara finished. "I don't think he killed Joe, I think Kevin did, but Jake was there when it happened. I have no doubt about that."

"Well, it's no wonder you reacted the way you did when you found out he was being so smug about it." Chuck paused and looked over at her. "I just wonder what you would've done had you been alone in that kitchen with him."

She narrowed her eyes at him. "What are you implying?"

He shrugged and looked away as a smile cracked his face. "I mean, you did pick up a knife."

"Oh, come on, I was just trying to scare him," she scoffed. "I wasn't going to stab him or anything."

He laughed. "I'm just joshing you," he said.

With that, the conversation changed direction. Under the moon and stars, they discussed their time at camp, and their futures. Chuck told her how excited he was to finally be an official veterinarian. Sara told him her aspirations to be a teacher. She'd just started college and had a couple of years to go. They each talked about what they wanted in life and Chuck was pleased to hear that they had a lot of common interests. Finally, when it seemed they'd talked about every subject imaginable, they realized it was deep into the night. Chuck looked back toward the dining hall and the cabins and discovered there wasn't a light on in any of the buildings.

"Wow, how long have we been out here," he asked, thinking aloud.

Sara looked at her watch. She had to position it just right to catch the moonlight so she could see. "Chuck it's already past midnight," she said with a giggle. "I can't believe we've been sitting out here talking this long."

"Me either," he said, and he started to get up.

"What are you doing?" she asked, grabbing his arm.

He looked at her, confused. "Sara, it's late. Don't you think we should get to bed?"

She shook her head. "No," she answered. "I don't want this night to end. Let's stay right here just a little while longer."

Chuck smiled at her. He couldn't believe how well this night was going and truthfully, he didn't want it to end either.

"Okay," he said, sinking back down beside her.

With his arm around her, they sat for a long time just watching the night sky. The gentle sound of water lapping under the pier and the occasional hoot of a night owl was all it took to eventually lull them into a deep sleep.

It was screaming that woke them.

Chuck sat up abruptly, surprised to find that the morning sun had just appeared over the treetops, and he could feel the warmth of it beginning to wash over him. For a moment, he wondered if he was dreaming. He looked around in all directions and could not find the source of the screaming.

"What is happening?" Sara said groggily as she sat up.

"Something's wrong," Chuck said. "Come on, hurry."

They both scrambled to their feet and began running up the hill toward the cabins. As they drew closer, it became apparent that the screaming was coming from not just a single person, but multiple people. It was coming from the children.

They ran past the cabins and Chuck noticed in the distance that all of the children seemed to be congregated in the playground. When they'd almost reached them, they noticed something that made them both gasp and almost stop dead in their tracks. A couple of the children appeared to have blood on their clothing and hands.

"What happened?" Chuck asked, doing his best to not sound panicked.

"They're dead!" a little boy called out. His Howdy Doody t-shirt was bloody.

"What?" Sara asked, a tremor in her voice. "Who is dead?"

"All of the counselors are dead!" another girl's voice called out, quaking. "We tried to w-wake them but they're not asleep or hurt–they're d-dead!"

More children began to cry. Some called out for their mothers. Most started begging to go home.

"It's okay, it's going to be okay," Chuck said, again forcing himself to keep a calm, steady voice. "Tell me where they are."

The little boy pointed toward the dining hall. "We went for breakfast when no one came to get us," he said frantically. "They're all dead and bloody in there!"

Chuck looked over at Sara. "Stay with them, do what you can to calm them down."

She glared at him, clearly concerned. "Chuck, do you really think you should go in there? We need to call the police!"

"I will, I will," he said reassuringly. "But let me check this out and get a better understanding of what the hell is going on."

Chuck sprinted to the entrance of the dining hall. He grabbed the handle, took a deep breath, and pulled the door open. What he saw inside made his knees buckle under him. He grabbed the door to steady himself and stared at the scene to make sure what he was seeing was actually real. The bodies of every single counselor–save he and Sara–were laid out on tables throughout the room. The top of every skull had seemingly been lopped off, exposing the brain. Chuck willed himself to move closer and when he did, he discovered many of the bodies had other injuries too. Some, like Julie Davis, had their throats slashed. Others seemed to have stab wounds peppered across their torsos. In the case of Jake Simpson, his stomach had been cut wide open to the point his entrails were clearly visible.

Chuck had never seen anything like this before but deduced from how the bodies were arranged that they'd perhaps been killed elsewhere in the camp and then brought into the dining hall. He wondered to himself if the tops of their skulls had been removed here, after they were dead.

Suddenly Chuck felt himself feeling very ill and before he knew it, he was retching on the floor. After he'd expelled his last meal, he hurried back out of the building and found Sara headed his way.

"Stop!" he said sharply. "Don't come over here!"

"Why?" she asked, her voice breaking into pieces. "What happened?"

"Stay with the kids," he said. "I'm headed to the office. I need a phone."

"What happened?" she repeated, her voice becoming shriller.

"They're dead," he said as he walked away. "All of them are dead."

Chuck made the call. He felt like a zombie when he did his best to explain what had happened. It was as if someone else was in control of his body, his voice, and he was a spectator watching and listening to everything as it unfolded. The sheriff's deputy that took the call was professional, but ultimately the concern in his voice was evident. The deputy told Chuck someone would be there within ten minutes and instructed him to keep himself and everyone else at the playground until help arrived. Chuck assured him that he would, and then woefully wandered back to where Sara and the children were gathered.

"Help is coming," he said, his voice monotone. "The police said we need to stay put right here until they get here."

Sara nodded in acknowledgement, but he could still see fear in her eyes.

"It's going to be okay," he said, doing his best to console her. "Whoever did this is gone. The deputy said they'll be here in ten minutes, tops."

Sara's arms were crossed, and she held herself tightly. It was then that Chuck noticed it wasn't just fear in her eyes, there was something else.

"Are you okay?" he asked.

She shook her head and motioned for him to follow her toward a secluded section of the playground near the see-saws. When they were out of earshot from the children she said, "Some of the kids are telling me some crazy stuff, Chuck."

He glanced back at the children, most of which were seated on and around the merry-go-round. "What kind of stuff?" he asked.

Sara's eyes darted around, and she shrugged. "I don't know what to make of it," she said. "They're saying they saw...something."

Chuck chuckled nervously. "Well, I'd say we've all seen something this morn–"

"No," she interjected. "Some of the kids saw someone wandering around the dining hall."

He stared at her, half excited, half bewildered. "You mean they saw the killer?"

She sighed and hugged herself tighter. "I'm not sure," she replied. "They said it was a monster with yellow eyes. One of the kids said it stood like a person but was covered in green slimy stuff and looked wet. What was described sounded kinda like pond sludge we've seen on the backs of the turtles in the lake."

Chuck swallowed and again looked over toward the children. They were all staring back at him, many of their faces still ashen with fear.

"Do you believe them?" he asked, looking back at Sara.

She sighed again. "I don't know, but again, multiple kids were telling me the same thing. So, I don't know, maybe."

"Maybe someone had been hiding out in the lake," he replied, trying desperately to come up with a logical explanation.

"What if it was Joe Folsom?" Sara asked abruptly.

The question caught Chuck completely off guard. He opened his mouth to quickly dismiss the notion but closed it almost just as fast. Could it really be him, he wondered. As he thought back to everything Sara had told him the night before, it was indeed true that Joe had more motive to do the heinous act than anyone else; but Joe had also been presumed dead.

"Joe's dead," he said softly as he stared out at the calm lake. "Ghosts can't kill people."

Even as he said the words, he wasn't entirely sure he still believed them.

Chapter Two

Friday, July 22, 1983

Brian Lancaster's mood shifted from excited to angry in record time. Mere minutes earlier he'd been envisioning how the night was going to go, literally rehearsing it in his head as if it were the script for a movie. The excitement of finally getting the opportunity he'd been waiting for made him feel like he was walking on a cloud of air. Dana Berkley, the absolute girl of his dreams, would be attending the same party he would be at later that night. But this wasn't just any party, this was the twenty-fifth anniversary of the camp counselor slayings that occurred at Camp Beaver Brook back in 1958. There were only a few other people that Brian knew about that would be showing up. Meeting up with other kids from high school at the ruins of the old summer camp sounded like a blast all by itself, but coupled with the news that Dana would be attending as well sounded almost too good to be true. He'd wondered if there was anything that could completely derail his plans, and then, as if the universe had been listening, he was delivered the answer, and it was a resounding 'yes'.

"Brian, do I detect a bit of sulking coming from your general direction?"

"No, Aunt Sara," he answered sharply.

"Well, your tone seems to suggest otherwise," she shot back.

Brian and his younger brother, Barry, had been staying with their aunt and uncle while their parents were away on a trip to Europe for their twentieth wedding anniversary. The boys loved staying with them, mostly due to the fact that their Uncle Chuck was a veterinarian and often paid them to help him take care of animals during their summer break from school. Their Aunt Sara was an accountant and did her work from home most days. For the most part, Brian thought his aunt and uncle were cool, at least as far as adults go, but there were moments where they seemed stricter than his parents. This was one of those moments.

"It's just that I had plans tonight," he replied. "Literally any other night would've been just fine, but not this one."

They were standing in the kitchen. Aunt Sara had been washing dishes while Brian poured himself a glass of orange juice from the refrigerator. She grabbed a dish towel, dried her hands and followed him over to the table where they both sat down.

"So, tell me about these plans," she said as she moved a strand of brown hair out of her face. She was in her early fifties now, and her hair was beginning to gray. She'd considered dying it but hadn't gotten up the nerve yet.

"Just a party with some friends," he answered wistfully. "I haven't seen most of them since school ended for summer break."

Aunt Sara chuckled. "You say that like it's been a year or something," she muttered. "And even if your Uncle Chuck and I didn't need you to watch Barry while we attend the memorial service tonight, I don't know that we'd be okay with you going to a party. What would your mom and dad say about that? Do they let you go to parties?"

Brian took a sip of orange juice and then let the question hang in the air a beat before finally saying, "All the time."

She shook her head. "Don't ever play poker, Brian," she shot back. "Even Stevie Wonder can see through that lie."

Brian huffed and shook his head. "I'm seventeen now," he said as if that would make all the difference.

"You've been seventeen for about five minutes," Aunt Sara replied.

It was true, Brian thought. He'd only turned seventeen the week before. For some reason he'd envisioned his life changing a lot when he hit that magic number. He believed people would start treating him more like an adult and, perhaps more importantly, adults would begin to trust him more. He quickly learned that was not the case at all.

"Tell you what," she said, seemingly reading his thoughts. "How about when Uncle Chuck gets home, I'll get him to give you some cash. Why don't you take your brother to see the new *Jaws* movie tonight while we're gone?"

Brian started to protest the idea because, party or no party, he had no desire to hang out with Barry away from home. But then, an idea crept into his mind that made him grin. He hoped the Cheshire cat smile wouldn't betray him.

"That's not a bad idea," he said, doing his best to not sound enthusiastic. "We do love those movies, and this one's supposed to be in 3-D."

"I heard that too," Aunt Sara said, her face lighting up. "You know when me and your Uncle Chuck were your age, 3-D movies were very popular. Maybe they're making a comeback?"

Brian just shrugged and finished his orange juice as he began to work out the logistics of his plan in his head. Half an hour later, Chuck came home, and Sara filled him in on her idea. Brian watched carefully to see how he would react.

"Are you sure we can trust you?" he asked, suspiciously.

Brian nodded. "Of course you can, Uncle Chuck."

Chuck pulled out his wallet and retrieved a twenty-dollar bill. He held it out but snatched it back just as Brian was about to grab it.

"You're not going to that party at the old Beaver Brook Campground tonight by any chance, are you?" he asked suddenly.

Brian gulped and cleared his throat. "Party? What party?" he asked clumsily.

Chuck's eyes narrowed and Brian could see his hand visibly tighten around the twenty-dollar bill. "Follow me," he said, motioning toward the back porch.

Brian did as he was told and glanced over at Sara as he walked away. He expected her to give him a playful smile in return, so it was surprising to see such a worried expression on her face. He exited the house and as the screen door slammed behind him, Chuck took a seat in one of the two rocking chairs on the porch. He pointed to the other empty one. "Have a seat, Brian."

He did as he was told, the old chair creaking in protest as he did so.

"What do you know about the murders that occurred at Camp Beaver Brook in 1958?" Chuck asked very matter-of-factly.

Brian grabbed the arm rest and sighed as he pondered the question. "Not a whole lot," he answered after a few seconds. "I know that some teenagers were killed and that they never found out who did it," he answered.

Chuck nodded. His gaze was focused on the tree line behind the house. It was as if he was focused on something that only he could see. "That's right," he said. "What else do you know about it?"

Brian shrugged. "Well, I mean, I've heard the legend that everyone talks about."

"What legend?"

Brian chuckled. "Uncle Chuck, you know what I'm talking about."

Chuck nodded and took a deep breath. "Yeah, I think I do but I want you to say his name."

Brian's mouth formed a straight line. He wondered where this was going. "Mossback," he replied.

For the first time, Chuck broke his gaze away from the woods and turned to look at his nephew. "I take it you don't believe the rumors?"

Brian was taken aback. Of course he didn't believe the rumors, he thought to himself. But was Uncle Chuck trying to suggest that he did? He wasn't sure what to say, so he just shook his head.

Chuck laughed and began rocking the chair. "Of course you don't," he grumbled. "It seems every year that passes by less and less people believe in him."

"Are you saying that you do?" he blurted out without thinking.

"I sure do," Uncle Chuck shot back. "There's something I need to tell you, Brian," he said, his tone growing more serious. "Something I think you're finally old enough to hear."

Brian was intrigued. He turned in his chair to face his uncle. "I'm listening," he said.

"Your mom and dad may get mad at me for telling you, but I feel like you need to know," he continued. "I'd never tell you to lie to your mom and dad, but I don't recommend just volunteering this information to them either. Do you get my point?"

Brian smiled and nodded. "Just tell me," He said anxiously.

Chuck flashed a grin for the first time and Brian was glad to see it. He'd never seen his uncle so serious before.

"Alright, I'll just cut right to the chase," he said. "Brian, me and your Aunt Sara were camp counselors at Camp Beaver Brook. We were there the night of the killings."

Brian's mouth fell open. He couldn't believe what he'd just heard, and he stared at his uncle for a minute waiting for him to start laughing to indicate he was screwing with him. The laugh never came.

"We were the only two counselors that survived that night," he said. "All of the kids were okay, thank God, but what happened to our friends that night..."

His words trailed off like the memories in his head were transporting him through some portal to another time and place.

"Wow," Brian said softly. It was the only word he could muster in the moment, but it seemed to be enough to bring Chuck back.

"I've thought about that night probably every single day of my life since then," he said. "Whoever killed those counselors was eerily quiet about it."

"Do you have any idea who could have done it?"

Chuck looked over at him and nodded slowly. "Brian, I know who did it and so does your Aunt Sara. We've always known."

Brian sat up in his chair. "Well tell me," He said, his voice rising. "Who killed them?"

"I believe the boy that killed them used to go by the name Joe Folsom," he answered. "He was a Native American boy–Choctaw, I think. I thought Joe had been killed accidentally a couple of years before but now I'm not so sure."

"Uncle Chuck, what do you mean you 'thought he'd been killed'?"

"I mean exactly what you're thinking," he replied. "Joe supposedly died from an accident, but I later found out that there was a little more to it."

"More to his death?"

Chuck sighed, suddenly feeling reluctant. "The counselors that died in 1958 were all there when Joe was hurt. It's my understanding that they could've intervened; they could've stopped some of the terrible things that went on that day and ultimately could've prevented him from being hurt. I've always believed that Joe returned to carry out vengeance on everyone that had any part in what happened to him."

Brian sank back into the chair as he mulled over everything he'd been told. Finally, he asked, "Well how does Mossback play into all this?"

"I think that Joe is Mossback," Uncle Chuck replied. "I know what I'm going to say sounds absolutely crazy, but I've thought about this a lot over the years so hear me out, okay?"

Brian nodded. "Okay."

"There were a couple of kids that claimed they saw who killed the counselors that night," he began. "They described a being covered in green slime–like algae or some kind of scummy stuff you'd find at the bottom of a swamp. I realize young kids can have pretty wild imaginations, but multiple kids described the same thing." Chuck paused and looked up at the porch ceiling fan as it lazily spun overhead. He seemed to be contemplating his next words. After a full minute had passed, he continued. "Now I'm not a big believer in ghosts, or ghouls or any other supernatural junk, but I'll tell you what I've always kind of been open minded to."

"What's that?"

"Shamanism," he answered quickly. "The magic that some Native Americans believe in and practice."

Brian stared at him wide-eyed and waited for him to continue.

"I think that the Joe Folsom I once knew is indeed gone," he said. "However, I think his reanimated body still roams the forest surrounding Beaver Brook Lake as Mossback, still seeking vengeance. I think it's due to some sort of shaman or voodoo magic that we don't understand."

There was an awkward silence that hung in the air for half a minute as Brian pondered Uncle Chuck's wild theory. As outlandish as it sounded, he'd never known his uncle to ever tell him a lie and he'd never been known as untrustworthy.

"Assuming all this is true," he said carefully. "There's a part of this that doesn't make any sense."

"What part is that?" Uncle Chuck asked, genuinely interested.

"You keep talking about vengeance," Brian said. "If it really was Joe, I thought he got his vengeance. He killed all those counselors that had anything to do with what happened to him. Why would he still be out there looking for revenge?"

"Probably because he didn't get everyone that was involved," he replied flatly.

Brian swallowed and felt the blood drain from his face. "Oh my god," he said. "He's after you?"

Uncle Chuck rubbed at the back of his neck, clearly becoming more uncomfortable the deeper the conversation went. "I don't think it's me he's after," he said. "I wasn't there when he was killed, hurt, or whatever you want to call it."

"Then who was?"

His brow furrowed and he glanced over his shoulder to peer into the window behind them. Brian looked back too and they could both see Sara back at the sink, finishing up the dishes.

"You're kidding me," Brian said, glancing back over at his uncle wide-eyed. "Why didn't he get her too that night?"

"He didn't hurt her because she was not in her bed where she was supposed to be," he explained. "Your Aunt Sara was with me out on the pier that night. We fell asleep out there and I guess old Mossback never knew we were even there. Hell, had he found us, he may have gotten me too for all I know."

Brian quickly rehashed everything his uncle had just told him in his mind. When he'd finished, he looked over at Chuck. "How do I know you're not just trying to scare me?" he asked, a hint of skepticism in his tone.

The older man looked back at him, a bit confused. "You think I'm trying to scare you?" he asked gruffly. "Well let me clear that up for you right now. Hell yes I'm trying to scare you!"

It was Brian's turn to be confused. "I don't understand. You just made all that up to–"

"I didn't make anything up," Chuck snapped. "Everything I told you is the truth. I wanted you to know the truth and, yes, get scared, so you will keep yourself and Barry as far away from that party tonight as possible! Am I clear?"

Brian nodded. "Yes sir," he said. "But how do you even know about the party?"

Uncle Chuck sighed. "What do you think the memorial service we're going to tonight is for?"

Brian thought and felt a bit silly when it finally occurred to him. "For the counselors that were murdered?"

"It's been twenty-five years since that grisly tragedy," he answered, nodding. "Everyone in town that was around back when it happened is reminiscing about it. It's kind of like when J.F.K. was shot. People like to ask 'where were you' when it happened. You can imagine the faces I get when I tell people where I was when it happened."

Brian laughed at that, and then wondered if he should have.

"Anyway," Chuck continued. "I stopped by the grocery store to pick up a gallon of milk. I overheard a couple of the kids stocking shelves talking about a little get together they were planning on being at later tonight. One of them mentioned that it would be at Camp Beaver Brook."

Brian felt his heart rate increase. "I don't know anything about it," he lied.

Chuck glared at him suspiciously. "Brian, I don't care if you know about it," he said. "Just don't go to it." He suddenly held his hand out again. "Take this money and you and Barry have a good time. Aunt Sara and I are going to the memorial and I'm not sure how long we'll be out."

Brian took the bill. "Thanks Uncle Chuck." He rose from the chair and pulled open the screen door.

"Hey Brian," Chuck called out.

He paused and turned to look back at him.

"Don't mention any of this to your Aunt Sara. She gets emotional about this stuff."

He nodded.

"And Brian."

"Yes, Uncle Chuck?"

"You're a good kid. I love you."

"I love you too," he said, smiling. "See ya later."

Chapter Three

Though he'd never admit it to anyone, thirteen-year-old Barry Lancaster wanted to be just like his older brother, Brian. Brian was bigger, stronger, older, and on the verge of being done with high school. Brian was also a very good basketball player and Barry often found himself wondering why he never inherited any of the athletic prowess his brother had somehow been blessed with. Barry was; however, a straight A student and it was not lost on him that Brian had struggled a lot academically.

Despite all their differences, there was one thing that the both of them did enjoy quite a lot. Going to the cinema was an experience quite like no other. The smell of buttery popcorn, the loud, booming speakers, and the silver screen were a feast for the senses. The Lancaster brothers always seemed to want to go see the same types of movies. So, when Barry found out that Brian was taking him to see the premier of *Jaws 3-D*, he could hardly contain his excitement.

"Have you ever seen a 3-D movie before?" he asked his brother.

Brian was piloting his orange 1971 Ford Pinto down an old dusty road near the northern end of Duke County. He was traveling south in the direction of the largest town in the county, Darkwood.

"Nah, can't think of any," he replied, his eyes focused on the terrain ahead of him.

Houses on this particular road were few and far between. Had the sun already gone down, he wouldn't have chosen this particular route even though it was the fastest way. The Pinto was reliable enough but now that the car was over ten years old, Brian's trust in the vehicle could only go so far.

"Aunt Sara said that the shark is going to jump off the movie screen," Barry said. His gaze was fixed onto the pine trees that rushed by outside his window.

"Well, it'll be cool if that really happens," Brian replied. "But I'll believe it when I see it."

Barry looked over at him quickly, as if he'd had a sudden epiphone. "Brian, I think this is the first time we've ever gone to see a movie without a grown up with us."

Brian considered that and when he thought back realized it was indeed true. Normally, the only time Barry rode anywhere with just him was to school and back. Even then, it wasn't year-round. When basketball season was in full swing, Barry often rode the bus home instead.

"Well, depending on how you act tonight, it could be the only time," he shot back with a sneer.

"What's that supposed to mean?" Barry asked, now turning his entire body to look at him.

Brian snorted. "Barry, let's just say I didn't volunteer to babysit you tonight."

"First of all, I am not a baby," Barry shot back boldly. In his gut, the comments from his big brother hurt, but he wasn't about to let him know it. "Secondly, I didn't volunteer myself to go anywhere with you either!"

Brian lifted his foot off the accelerator, allowing the car to slow down. "Oh, are you saying you don't want to see the movie?"

Barry's eyes widened.

"Because I can turn this car around and we'll just sit at home and watch *The Dukes of Hazzard* tonight."

"No!" Barry said, probably with a tone of more desperation than he wanted. "I want to see this movie. I'm sorry."

Brian smirked and mashed the gas again. "Okay then," he replied. "Be a little more respectful to your elders."

Barry rolled his eyes and returned his attention to the trees that continued to whiz by. There was so much he wanted to say. If there was any other way, he could've gotten himself to the cinema, he'd have done it all by himself, he thought bitterly.

The Pinto topped a hill, and Brian was momentarily blinded by the sun, low in the western sky. He held a hand up to shield the blinding light and his eyes regained focus just as they came upon a car that was broken down on the side of the road. Brian swerved the car hard to the left to give the stranded motorist a wide berth. Once they were past, he glanced up at the rearview mirror to get a better look. When he realized who it was, his jaw dropped, and he slammed on the brakes. The Pinto skidded to a wild stop, nearly sideways, blocking both lanes of the road.

"What are you doing?" Barry hollered. "Are you crazy?"

He looked over at his brother and found him staring back at the car that was broken down on the side of the road. It was a sleek, blue 1975 Plymouth Fury. There was steam rising from the front of the vehicle's grille. Suddenly Barry realized it wasn't the car that Brian was staring at with lust in his eyes. It was the curly haired brunette leaning against the driver side door. She wore tight white shorts, a yellow blouse, and an expression comprised of a mixture of fear and anger all at once. Barry had just begun puberty, so it was very easy for him to understand Brian's sudden infatuation.

"That's Dana Berkley," Brian said wistfully.

Barry thought he could see literal hearts in his brother's eyes. He seemed distant, like he was in an entirely different place. "What about the other girl?"

Brian suddenly snapped back to reality. "Other girl?" he asked. He adjusted his vision back to the car and could see someone else inside. He immediately recognized her too. "That's Andi Parker," he said, annoyed. "Mark's girlfriend."

Mark Hopper was Brian's close friend and captain of the football team. He was a tall, blonde-haired, blue-eyed jock in every sense of the word. They'd been friends since the third grade but somehow had gotten even closer in high school. Brian suspected it had something to do with their interest, and dominance in their respective sports, Brian in basketball and Mark in football. The party at the Beaver Creek Campground had become known to Brian only because Mark had told him. Ever since Mark had discovered that Brian had an eye for Dana, he'd made it his personal mission to get the two of them together. It just so happened that Andi was also Dana's best friend. He'd never been very fond of her. Andi had a reputation around school that he was certain her parents would not be proud of. Her promiscuity also made him wary for the sake of his friend, Mark. She went through boyfriends like she went through Kleenex.

"Wait here," he said to Barry as he opened the driver's side door.

He slammed the door behind him, just as Barry had begun voicing his protest, and briskly walked toward the steaming vehicle.

"Do you need some help?" he asked Dana.

She smiled at him. "Brian, I'm so glad you came by," she said, meeting him at the front of the car. "I think the car overheated. I don't know what to do."

Andi opened the passenger side door and exited the vehicle. She, like Mark, was also blonde haired and blue eyed. She wore cut-off jean shorts and a bright red T-shirt that matched her lips. "Yes, thank God you showed up," she said, clearly agitated. "Mark is gonna hear an earful from me when I see him."

"Why?" Brian asked, innocently. "What did he have to do with this?"

Andi's jaw dropped, making it quite clear that she couldn't believe he had to gall to question her. Dana rolled her eyes where only Brian could see her.

"He could've picked us both up, but instead he elected to go get a haircut," she spat. "A haircut! Can you believe that? I had to call Dana to come and get me. If he'd have just come and gotten us this wouldn't have happened."

"He couldn't have known that Dana's car was going to break down," Brian rebutted, as gently as he could.

It was Andi's turn to roll her eyes. "Well, why don't you just become his boyfriend since you clearly love him so much," she snapped. "With the way I feel right now, I'm very much okay with cutting him loose so you can be with him."

Brian felt his face get hot, a combination of anger and embarrassment. He slowly glanced over at Dana. She awkwardly looked away and he could see she was stifling an amused smile. As much as he wanted to engage in a heated argument with Andi, he resisted the urge. Ultimately, he decided to focus his attention where he really wanted it, on Dana.

"It definitely looks like the car overheated," he said, looking over at the wisps of steam still rising from under the hood. "Let me take you where you're headed. After the car cools down later, I can help you get it going again," he said, trying to sound like he knew what he was talking about.

"You know where we're headed," Andi said. "Don't act like you're not headed there too."

"I don't think I'm going to make it," he said, still keeping his attention on Dana.

She frowned when he said it, a response that both surprised him and thrilled him all at the same time.

"Why aren't you coming?" she asked. "It's going to be a blast, Brian, you should come."

He swallowed, momentarily frozen and unsure how to respond. He couldn't believe Dana actually wanted him to be there.

"He's probably too scared," Andi said with a grin. "Are you scared Mossback will get you, Brian?"

He closed his eyes and shook his head. "No, it's not that at all," he said calmly. "It's just that–"

"Brian, what's taking so long?" Barry called out suddenly.

When Andi saw the younger Lancaster brother hanging out of the Pinto's passenger side window she began laughing. "Oh, I see," she said, cackling. "Brian's gotta babysit tonight. That's why he can't come."

He clasped the back of his neck and tried to keep Andi's big mouth from getting to him. "Yeah, I uh, I'm taking him to see a movie tonight," he said, directing the words to Dana only. "My aunt and uncle are going to the memorial tonight and asked me to watch him. So, yeah, I'm sorry, I just can't make it."

Dana's frown remained and she looked over at Barry. The younger boy was waving enthusiastically as if he knew something she did not. She then looked back to Brian and said, "Why don't you just bring him along?"

Andi immediately scowled at the suggestion. "Dana, are you serious? We don't need a kid hanging around there tonight!"

"I don't know," Brian said, ignoring Andi. "He's pretty excited about seeing the movie."

"What's his name?" Dana asked.

"Barry," he replied.

She shot him a mischievous smile and began marching toward Barry. "Hey Barry," she said when she drew close to him. "Instead of that movie tonight, how would you like to come hang out with me and my friends for a little while?"

The expression on Barry's face immediately clouded when he heard the proposition. Brian could see that the question had flustered his younger brother, probably because it was coming from such a pretty girl.

"I don't know," he said meekly. "I mean, I guess I'll do whatever Brian wants to do."

Great, Brian thought. He hadn't forgotten his promise to Uncle Chuck and up until now, Barry provided a nice excuse to stay away from the Beaver Brook Campground.

"I thought you had your heart set on the movie," he shot back.

Barry shrugged. "Brian, we can go see it another time," he replied. Barry may have been young, but he wasn't stupid. It was very obvious to him that his older brother had a massive crush on Dana. Who was he to get in the way of that? If he could help his brother out, he was more than willing to do it.

"At this point, I don't care who goes and who stays," Andi said, still making no attempt to hide her clear annoyance. "I'm tired of sitting on the side of the road. The sun is going down so are we going or not?"

Brian sighed, now realizing that he was at a crossroads. He could either give in and take Barry with him to the party–which was ultimately what he really did want to do; or he could stand his ground and tell the girl that he was infatuated with that he still felt it was best to skip the party and go to *Jaws 3-D* with Barry. That, of course, was what Uncle Chuck and Aunt Sara would want him to do.

"Give me just a minute," he said as he briskly walked over to the passenger side of the Pinto and leaned close to Barry so only his brother could hear him. "If we do this, you can't say a word to anyone about it," he whispered. "Do you understand that?"

Barry nodded, his eyes wide with excitement.

"Are you okay with that?"

Barry nodded again. "Yeah, I'll keep quiet about it, I promise." He pinched two fingers together and ran them across his lips, simulating the act of closing a zipper.

Brian nodded and directed his gaze again at Dana. The golden light from the setting sun washed over her, making her almost glow. She was always a looker, but he'd never thought she looked quite as gorgeous as she did in that particular moment. *There's nothing else to consider*, he thought.

"Alright," he said to them. "Andi, you and Barry get in the back. Dana, you can ride shotgun."

Dana smiled and clapped happily. Andi rolled her eyes again at the notion of her being assigned to the backseat with a kid. Within minutes they all climbed into the Pinto and were on their way to whatever was left of Camp Beaver Brook.

Chapter Four

"We're getting close," Andi said, as she leaned forward between Brian and Dana. "The driveway to the camp is an old gravel road. No one ever goes down it, so the woods are really grown up around it. If you're not paying attention, you'll miss it."

Brian slowed the Pinto and watched the right side of the road very carefully. He'd driven down this particular road many times before and never recalled seeing another road branch off of it.

"Are you sure?" he asked, squinting. "I don't see a road."

"It's here, keep looking," Andi snapped curtly.

He glanced over at Dana. "Have you ever seen this road?"

She shrugged. "No, but I've never looked for it either," she replied.

"There it is. Stop!" Andi shouted.

Brian slammed on the brakes. Andi's forehead slammed into the back of Dana's seat, and she cursed. "You idiot, do you know how to drive?" she hissed while rubbing her head.

"You're sure this is it?" Brian asked, ignoring her insult. He stared at the remnants of an old two track that, in his mind, barely qualified as a road. The thick trees and shrubbery on either side of it hung over, threatening to swallow up anyone that dared to venture in. Brian figured in the wintertime the road would be much easier to travel when all the vegetation died down.

"Yes, I'm positive," Andi answered, still massaging her forehead. "It clears out a lot once you get away from the main road."

"Are you sure?" he asked, still skeptical. "I'm not sure this car will make it very far."

Andi huffed. "Oh my god, are you always such a pansy?" she asked. "Why in the hell is Mark friends with you?"

"Brian, it's up to you," Dana said, herself sounding a bit unsure.

He glanced into the rearview mirror to try and get a glimpse of Barry. His younger brother locked eyes with him and smiled, seemingly completely oblivious to any of his concerns.

"What do you want to do?" he asked, returning his attention to Dana.

She pursed her lips and stared at the dark shadows beyond the foliage. "I mean, we can try," she said hopefully. "If we find out that it's not safe, maybe then we could wait for George. He's got a four-wheel drive."

Brian winced. "George Valentine is coming too?" he asked.

Dana nodded. "Yes, is that okay?" she asked, noticing his reaction to the news.

Brian forced a smile. "Of course it's okay," he said, doing his best to hide his displeasure. The truth was that he really didn't have any issues with George Valentine. He was a good guy and a heck of a baseball player. The two of them had never been close but were always cordial. What he did have an issue with was the fact that it had become known to him at the end of the previous school year that George too had his eye on Dana. Brian felt that if he had a night with Dana to himself, maybe he could get a leg up on any impending attempts George was going to make to woo her.

"Are you sure?" Dana asked, seemingly seeing past his charade.

Brian felt his face get hot. "Yes, of course I'm sure," he said, desperately wanting to change the subject.

"I doubt that George would be hesitating right now," Andi said, taking full advantage of the awkward situation.

Brian's fake smile quickly vanished, and he bit his lip to avoid saying something he would potentially regret. Instead, without speaking another word, he steered the Pinto onto the road and carefully maneuvered the car through the narrow opening. As they advanced along the two track, he could hear low limbs rubbing crudely across the top of the car and wondered if the paint was getting scratched. He thought of Mark's Thunderbird. That car was the most important thing in the world to him. Surely he wouldn't risk putting the car through this sort of terrain, Brian thought.

He was pleasantly surprised to find that what Andi had told him turned out to actually be true. The further they ventured into the woods, the better the road became. Soon the shrubs and trees that had clung to the Pinto, as if they were trying to keep them from arriving at Camp Beaver Brook, all but disappeared. The two track had high grass along its center but otherwise, the road was relatively smooth considering how long it had probably been since another vehicle had used it.

"Look at that," Dana said, pointing at the arched entrance ahead.

Andi and Barry both went for the space between the front seats and after a brief shoving match, Andi prevailed and claimed the spot. "It's crazy that after all these years and, after all the stories we've heard, that now we can see it is actually real," she said.

Brian leaned over the steering wheel and peered up at the ominous sign as they traveled under it. It had apparently been made of metal, and he could tell at one time it had been a brilliant shade of blue, evidenced by the bits of peeling paint that still hung on. Now it was mostly the color of rust. Beyond the archway, what appeared to be a parking lot opened up in front of them with a large building beside it. On the side of the wooden structure a sign hung sideways, apparently being held on by a single nail in one corner, with the words DINING HALL scrawled on it. On the other side of the parking lot were the remnants of an old playground, containing a tall metal slide, a jungle gym, merry-go-round and dangling chains that once were attached to swings.

Brian brought the car to a stop in the center of the parking lot and the four of them clambered out.

"This doesn't seem so scary," Andi said, placing her hands on her hips as she scanned over the environment.

"We're the first ones here," Dana said, as she too surveyed her surroundings. "That's great, we've got time to explore it all before anyone else shows up!"

Andi smiled at the suggestion. Brian was considering how he could protest the idea when he noticed Barry had sprinted directly to the playground.

"Barry, get back over here," he said. "That stuff is so ancient, you're gonna get cut and need a tetanus shot!"

Barry completely ignored his brother and began climbing the ladder on the slide. Brian noticed beyond the playground and down the hill there was a large lake with a rickety pier. "Hey, that's pretty cool," he said, pointing.

The girls looked, noticed the lake, and then began running toward it.

"Hey, be careful, don't go out on that pier!" he called out. Brian sighed as it became apparent, they were ignoring him. As he trailed after them, he began to feel as if he were the most responsible person present at the moment. It wasn't a feeling he was very thrilled to have.

"I wonder if there are any fish in there." Dana said as she stopped near the water's edge.

"There's bound to be a few," Brian said as he peered into the murky water.

Andi's eyebrows raised and she said, "Oh, I bet there's at least one dead body somewhere in there too."

"Probably," Dana agreed with a giggle. "And I'm pretty sure Mossback is lurking somewhere out there."

Andi flashed a mischievous smile at Dana. "There's only one way to find out," she said.

Dana frowned. "No, Andi, don't," she replied, her eyes pleading.

Andi shook her head and then took off running. As soon as she made it onto the pier, she peeled her shirt off, throwing it wildly into the air behind her.

"Andi, no!" Brian yelled, but it was a futile plea.

Andi reached the end of the pier and jumped high into the air, immediately pulling her knees to her now bare chest to make a cannonball. She squealed with delight as she plunged into the lake causing a large splash.

Dana crossed her arms and shook her head. "I cannot believe she actually just did that," she said.

"Me either," Brian said, a bit gob smacked. He couldn't decide what shocked him more, the fact that she'd so carelessly jumped into a lake that they knew nothing about, or how she'd just exposed her breasts to him so easily.

Andi's head suddenly popped up from the water and she began doing the backstroke, again with no regard for her topless state.

Brian looked away, embarrassed. "Dana, please tell her to get out of there and to put her shirt back on," he said anxiously.

Dana laughed. "Oh, come on, Brian," she replied. "What? Are you the only boy in school that hasn't seen Andi's boobs?"

"You tramp, I heard that!" Andi called out from the lake. "Tell Mr. Modest that I'm under the water again so he can look."

Brian looked back toward her and was relieved to find that she was indeed covered again by the dark water. "It's not me," he said, doing his absolute best to not sound so embarrassed. "It's Barry. He's a little kid and doesn't need to be seeing this."

Andi rolled her eyes and then ran her hands over her soaking wet hair. "Whatever," she muttered dismissively. "Barry is up there on the jungle gym paying us no attention."

"Yeah, but he could come down here any minute," Brian rebutted.

"Brian's right, Andi," Dana said. "Barry doesn't need to be seeing you like that. Get out of there and put your shirt back on. Besides, there could be snakes in there!"

Andi rolled her eyes again. Brian was beginning to wonder how many times a day she did that.

"Y'all are absolutely no fun," she said as she began to swim back toward the shore.

Brian prepared to turn his back again to avoid seeing her when suddenly he heard her gasp. "What's wrong?" he called out.

"I don't know," she replied, sounding a bit worried. "Something just touched my leg."

Dana stepped toward the water. "What did you just say?" she asked, her voice raising an octave.

"You heard me," Andi shot back. Suddenly she jerked to the side as if she were trying to move away from something. "Oh my god," she squealed. "There it was again. Something is touching my leg!"

"Well, what are you waiting for?" Brian said, a bit frantic now. "Get out of the water!"

There was fear in Andi's eyes when they locked with Brian's. She began quickly swimming toward the shore.

"Hurry!" Dana shouted.

Andi had barely moved when she screamed again. Suddenly, she disappeared beneath the water.

"Oh my god," Dana screamed. "What's happening?"

"Andi!" Brian yelled. "Andi, get out of there!"

Her head popped up again and her screams continued. "Something has my ankle!" she said, her words garbled with water. "Please help me!"

Brian looked on, his heart now beating to the point where he thought it would jump out of his chest. Without thinking he began sprinting up the pier until he was alongside her. He jumped into the water and immediately went under, reaching out for her. Luckily, he found her arm almost instantly. He pulled her to him and used all the strength he could muster to swim with his free arm toward the shore. She squealed again, and he wondered if whatever was in the water was biting her or perhaps worse. Finally, his foot found the bottom and then he was able to drag her to land, collapsing from exhaustion the moment he reached it.

Brian was drenched, and he heaved as he tried to get his breath back while his heart continued to beat rapidly. He couldn't remember the last time he'd been so scared. He turned to check on Andi just as Dana reached them and it was then that he realized things were not at all as they seemed. Andi wasn't squealing from pain or fear, she was squealing with laughter. She had curled into the fetal position and was laughing so hard he thought she was going to pass out. Dana had draped her shirt over her and shot Brian an apologetic look.

"What are you doing?" he asked, riddled with confusion.

When Andi had finally regained some level of composure, she said, "You really thought I was in trouble?"

He glared at her as the reality of it all began to set in. "Yeah," he said flatly. "I did."

She giggled as she pulled her shirt back on. "I can't believe you fell for that so easily," she said. "I never expected you to jump into the lake!"

The mere mention of what had just transpired made her start laughing again as she seemingly replayed it in her mind. "You just jumped right in!"

Brian clenched his jaw, stood up, and then stormed away back up the hill. He heard Dana call after him, but he was too enraged to look back at her. Barry met him as he reached the top.

"What happened to you?" he asked, peering at his brother's wet clothes.

"None of your business," Brian snapped without even looking at him. He reached the entrance to the dining hall only to find it locked. He was so angry; he took a step back and then kicked the door hard enough to break it loose. The doors flailed open wildly, setting off a cloud of dust in their wake. He marched toward the kitchen, hoping there would be some sort of towel, or even paper towels, in there that he could use to dry off. The kitchen looked very much like something he'd seen in an old black and white movie. The tiled floor was some ugly color he could only guess was some shade of aqua. The walls were covered in painted wooden paneling, though the white paint was peeling very much the way he'd noticed on the arched sign when they entered the property. He noticed a stack of old newspapers in one corner of the room. One wall was covered with stacked wooden chairs. The counters and shelves in the place were for the most part barren, but he did observe several dead insects, cobwebs and a thick layer of dust. On the wall above the counter nearest him hung several kitchen knives; one of them was particularly large like the one he'd seen Michael Myers wield in *Halloween*.

On another wall he saw a doorway with a sign above it indicating that it was a restroom. He made his way inside and was relieved to find several rolls of old toilet paper stacked on a shelf over the sink.

"Bingo," he said, as he then pulled off his shirt which he then began wringing out over the sink. He tossed the now damp, not sodden, garment over the side of a stall. Suddenly Dana appeared in the doorway.

"I'm so sorry about that," she said quickly.

Brian sighed and waved her off. "No need to apologize," he muttered. "Not your fault."

"Then why do I feel like it is?" she asked, crossing her arms.

He shrugged as he began unfurling the roll of toilet paper around his hand. When he had a large wad of paper, he began dabbing away the moisture from his body. "I don't know," he answered. "I guess because she's an ass, but she's also your friend, and we all have some control when we pick our friends."

She frowned and nodded sadly. "I suppose that's true," she said. "For what it's worth, I was really impressed with what you did. That was very brave of you."

Brian smiled, despite himself. It was hard to continue to be angry after hearing Dana make a statement like that. "I appreciate that," he said, doing his best to refrain from displaying a goofy grin.

"And I told her she needed to apologize to you," Dana continued. "She knows that I didn't like it either and she finally told me she was sorry, but I don't want her apology. I told her to save it for you, not me."

"Thanks for saying that," he said. "But I won't hold my breath."

"Anyway, I think maybe we could find an old camp t-shirt or something around here that you could wear instead of the wet shirt."

"Maybe," Brian muttered. "Again, I won't hold my breath on that either. Judging from what I saw in the kitchen and dining area, this place was pretty well cleaned out back when it was closed."

"Maybe Mark or George will have another shirt when they get here," she said confidently. "Yes, I'm sure they'll probably have something."

"We'll see," he replied. He threw the wet piles of toilet paper into an old beat-up garbage can in the corner of the bathroom and grabbed his damp shirt. "I guess we should get back out there. I don't trust Andi alone with Barry."

Dana's eyes widened as she seemed to conjure up some distressing scenarios in her mind's eye. "Yeah, you're right," she conceded. "Let's go."

They made their way back through the dining hall to exit the building and Brian noticed there were large brown stains on the tiled floor.

Could that be blood?

Chapter Five

"I'm sorry," Andi said.

Brian couldn't believe she actually said it. He also couldn't believe that it sounded genuine.

"Seriously," Andi said as she seemed to read the skepticism on his face. "I was just having a little fun, but I truly never meant for you to jump in after me. Dana told me how it all appeared and, what can I say, I had no idea I was that good of an actress. All in all, I think it was pretty sweet of you to do what you did."

He stared at her, looking for any hint of a lie in her face. He couldn't find one. "I appreciate it," he said. "Now let's forget it."

"You can make it up to him by helping us find a dry shirt around here," Dana said, peering at the cabins behind the dining hall.

The cabins were all made of logs and had wooden shingles on the roofs. One of them had a fallen tree on top of it that looked as if it had been there for at least the past ten years. There was a path dividing them all with four cabins on the left side, and four on the right (including the one destroyed by the fallen tree). There was no more than twenty feet of space between each one.

"I'm guessing the girl cabins were on the right, and the boy cabins were on the left," Andi said as she examined them all from afar.

"How in the world would you possibly know that?" Dana asked.

"Just a hunch," she answered as she began to make her way toward the row of cabins on the right. The girls are going to search the right, while you boys search the left."

Brian looked at Dana and shrugged. Frankly, he didn't care who searched which cabins. "Just be careful," he told them as he motioned for Barry to follow him.

They entered the first cabin they came upon, designated with a large letter A carved from wood and nailed on the wall beside the front door.

"I guess it's safe to assume this is Cabin A," Brian said as he reached for the doorknob. He twisted it and fully expected it to be locked. To his surprise, the knob turned with ease and the door swung open.

"Wow," Barry said, darting past him. "It looks like this place was left just the way it was back in the fifties."

"Get back here," Brian said, grabbing his brother's shoulder and pulling him back. "Let me check things out first." He moved past Barry and surveyed his dust-covered surroundings. Unlike the dining hall, the cabin he was now standing in appeared to still have all the contents it had contained twenty-five years ago.

There were four bunk beds against two walls that still had disheveled linens and pillows on each mattress. In the center of the wood-planked floor there was a large rug with the letters CBB, and a smiling beaver embroidered on it. On one wall, and placed under a window, was a desk with a notepad and pencil lying on it. Brian walked over for a closer look and found that a note had been scrawled on the paper. The handwriting looked like that of a child and after reading the first few lines he quickly determined it was the beginning of a letter that was intended to be sent to the child's parents. It read:

Dear Mom and Dad, Camp Beaver Brook is a lot of fun. There is so much to do here and I'm having a great time! Yesterday I rode in a canoe across the lake. Today I painted a birdhouse and hung it from a tree. We are waiting to see if a bird will live in it. Most of the counselors are nice but there is one named Jake that isn't nice. He is always yelling. Some of the kids told me that they saw a monster in the woods last night, but I think they were just trying to scare me. My leg has been itching a lot, and I think I may have poison ivy. One of the counselors named Sara gave me some cream for it and it is helping. Anyway I can't wait to...

The letter ended abruptly as if the writer had paused with the intent to come back and finish it later. The kid had mentioned 'Sara', and he immediately wondered if this was a reference to his Aunt Sara. There was also a mention of a 'monster' in the woods, and he couldn't help but think about Mossback.

"Cool," Barry said, again darting past his brother. Brian looked on as he picked up a football lying on the floor, but his joy turned to disappointment when he realized that the ball was deflated.

Brian set his gaze on a bookshelf on one of the walls and marveled at the small collection of classic tomes.

"It's like we've gone back in time or something," he said wistfully.

He then made his way over to the closet, opened the door and was shocked to find exactly what he'd been looking for. There were three Camp Beaver Brook t-shirts hanging there, yellow with brown lettering and the image of the same smiling beaver he'd noticed on the rug. Brian snatched the largest one off the hanger and shook it hard to make sure there were no spiders inside it. The cloud of dust produced by his action made him sneeze. Brian pulled the shirt over his head and noticed it smelled slightly of mildew, but it was dry and, in the moment, that mattered more to him.

He turned to leave the cabin and noticed Barry fiddling with something he'd gotten off of a small corner table. "What have you got now?" he asked.

Barry faced him, snatching his hands back as if he'd been caught doing something criminal. "Nothing," he muttered.

Brian approached and pushed his brother aside to reveal an old Swiss Army Knife lying on the table. He picked it up, immediately noticing that Barry had just enough time to open the screwdriver tool before being seen.

"What is it?" Barry asked.

Brian shook his head and laughed. "Seriously? You've never seen one? It's a Swiss Army Knife," he muttered. "And this thing is in mint condition."

He opened all of the tools, examining them all before eventually closing the knife and dropping it into his pocket. "Definitely taking this with me," he said. "Let's go find the girls."

They stepped back outside and began trotting down the front steps when suddenly they heard the sound of glass shattering in the next cabin. Barry stopped dead in his tracks and looked back at Brian.

"Did you hear that?"

Brian nodded.

"How about that, I see you found a shirt!" Dana called out suddenly.

Brian whipped his head around and found her and Andi approaching from the other row of cabins. He immediately held a finger up to his mouth. Andi opened her mouth, probably to argue, but quickly snapped it shut when they all began hearing the sound of footsteps in the cabin now.

"Who is that?" Dana whispered, glaring at Cabin B frightfully.

Brian shrugged and kept staring at the window nearest him for any sign of movement. Part of him wanted to run away. The other part saw the moment as yet another opportunity to impress Dana. Of course, impressing her wouldn't matter if he were dead. Without giving the matter much thought, he reached into his pocket and retrieved the knife he'd just found. He pulled the 3-inch blade open and held it in front of him as he approached Cabin B.

"Stay here," he whispered to the others.

Carefully, and as quietly as he could, he ascended the four steps that led to the front porch. With the knife still held in front of him, he called out, "Hey! Who's in there?"

No response.

"I'm not messing around," he said, making sure to keep his voice stern. "I've got a knife."

With his free hand he slowly reached for the knob and grabbed it. As was the case with Cabin A, the door was unlocked and the knob twisted with ease. Brian allowed the door to creak open and when he could finally see all of the interior, he squinted and tried to make out any movement in the shadows. When he saw none, he stepped inside, still allowing the knife to lead the way. He had taken only three steps when he heard something crunch beneath his sneakers. Brian looked down and saw that he'd just stepped into a pile of broken glass. To the left of the glass was the base of a lantern.

The glass came from the lantern, he thought. Suddenly, he heard the door behind him creak to life and looked back just in time to see it slam shut, trapping him inside.

Outside, Dana screamed. Andi cursed and turned to run away, knocking Barry down as she did so. Barry called out to Brian and scrambled to his feet. Dana grabbed him around the waist before he could run to the cabin.

"Don't," she said in a shriek. "We don't know who is in there!"

The sound of a muffled shout came from inside the cabin.

"Brian!" Barry yelled, still trying to pull himself free of Dana's grasp. "Let me go!"

The door suddenly jerked open and almost immediately, Barry felt relief. Brian appeared in the doorway, and he was laughing. Alongside him, there were two other boys his age, both of which he recognized. On Brian's right stood Carl Leonard, star running back for the varsity football team. On the left was Mark Hopper, the team quarterback and Brian's best friend since they were in elementary school. Both boys had their arms draped around Brian's neck and all three were smiling.

"That's the second time I've been duped today," Brian said as he led the trio outside.

"I don't know that my heart can take much more of this," Dana replied, exasperated.

Andi ran up to Mark and jumped into his arms. She wrapped her legs around him and grabbed him behind the head, pulling him to her for a kiss.

"Geez, get a room," Carl said, shaking his head. He was sporting gray sweats, the sleeves torn off the shirt. He walked over to Barry, put his large hand over the top of his head, and then proceeded to mess his hair up. Barry laughed.

Andi glared at Carl, not appreciating his comment at all but she said nothing and returned her attention to Mark. "What took you so long?" she asked, frowning.

"You know what took me so long, babe," he said, his eyes drifting upward to his hairline. "How does it look?"

She licked her lips as she looked him over. "It'll do," she muttered absently. "I really was mad at you for a little while because you have no idea what all I had to go through just to get here."

He stared at her, confused. "What happened?" he asked, and then, "Why is your hair wet?"

As Andi began her rant about how horrible things became for her when Dana's car broke down, Brian approached Carl and asked, "How did you guys sneak in here? Where did you park?"

Carl smiled and pointed to a narrow trail entrance behind the cabins.

"That trail leads to the back entrance," he said. "We drove up to the front entrance and Mark said there wasn't any way in hell he was going to take his car through all that mess. Then George chimed in and said there was a back entrance he knew about that we could get too off that old dirt road that leads to the power station."

"Oh really?" Brian asked, seeming to miss everything Carl had said except the part about George being there. "So, George rode in with y'all?"

Carl nodded. "Yep, we picked him up after his shift at the grocery store ended. You know the barbershop is right next to the grocery store so it kinda worked out."

"Right," Brian said, realizing that was indeed true. "Well, if he came with y'all, where is he?"

"He and Nicole took another trail to check out an old water tower that George has been going on about," Carl explained. "He said it was on the way in and not many people knew about it. Nicole wanted to see it, so they took a little detour."

Brian blinked at him. "Nicole?" he asked, confused.

"Nicole Phillips," Carl said. "You know, *Pac-Man* girl."

"Ah, okay," Brian said, suddenly knowing exactly who he meant. Fifteen year old Nicole Phillips was an arcade ace and her specialty was *Pac-Man*. She'd owned the high score at the Darkwood Arcade for at least the past two years.

"Nicole is here?" Barry said, suddenly perking up.

Brian smiled and leaned in close to Carl. "My kid brother has a massive crush on her," he whispered.

Carl's face split with a wide grin. He quickly turned to face Barry. "She sure is," he said. "You know Nicole?"

Barry's face turned pink. "Yeah," he said, rubbing at the back of his neck. "I mean, I talked to her a couple of times at the arcade. She's cool."

"Well, I guess since you two are the youngest here, y'all will probably hang out," Carl said, with a wink.

"Hey Brian!" Mark shouted. He sounded angry and he was marching toward him like he meant business.

"What is it?" Brian asked, confused by his aggressive tone and gait.

Mark gave him a hard look, his brow furrowed. "What's this crap Andi is telling me about you jumping in the lake with her when she was skinny dipping?"

Chapter Six

"Wait…what?" Brian asked as he tried to comprehend the bizarre accusation in his head.

"That's what she just told me," Mark growled, jerking a thumb over his shoulder toward Andi.

Brian gritted his teeth and glared at her. She smiled at him and batted her eyelashes theatrically.

"So, you're telling me you believe that's what happened?" he asked, his blood now boiling.

Mark stared at him but the hard lines on his face softened. "Well, I mean her hair is all wet and you've had to change shirts. Hell, your shoes are even wet. What am I supposed to think?"

Brian sighed. "Think whatever you want," he grumbled and walked away.

Carl looked over at Barry, wide eyed and clearly uncomfortable. "Hey, I got an idea," he said to Barry. "You want to go fishing?"

Barry lit up. "Heck yeah!"

Carl motioned for him to follow. "Come on," he said, and then turned to Mark who was still standing there watching Brian walk away. "We're heading back to the car to get the poles and tackle. I think we're gonna do a late evening fishing."

"Yeah, whatever," Mark said, shoving his hand in his pocket to retrieve the keys to the Thunderbird. He tossed them in the air, and Barry jumped up and caught them.

"Nice catch, kid," Carl said, slapping him on the back. "You should try out for wide receiver one day." The two of them disappeared into the forest leaving Mark, Andi, and Dana alone.

"What the hell is wrong with you," Dana said to Andi. "What are you trying to do?"

Andi shrugged. "I mean, I'm not lying, Dana," she replied slyly. "I took my shirt off for a swim and next thing I knew Brian was in the water with his arms around me."

Dana took a deep breath and shook her head. "I repeat, what the hell is wrong with you?"

"Are you saying she's lying?" Mark asked suddenly, stepping between them.

Dana glared at him, her brown eyes growing darker. "I'm saying there are some details your girlfriend is conveniently leaving out."

Mark looked over at Andi. "Babe, what is she talking about? What else happened?"

Andi screwed up her mouth. "Well, I may have been playing a little joke too," she said, raising her eyebrows.

Mark huffed and swallowed making it seem as though he'd been in situations similar to this before with Andi. "Did you do the stupid thing where you pretend to be drowning?" he asked.

"No," Dana answered. "She did the thing where she pretended like something had her by the leg and was trying to pull her under the water."

Mark slapped a hand to his forehead. "Andi," he said with exasperation. "You can be such a bi–

"Watch it," she snapped, cutting him off. She strode briskly to him and pushed her finger into his chest. "You call me that and I'll definitely turn into one for you."

Mark shook his head, gave her a blank stare, and then walked away.

"Where are you going?" she called after him.

"To apologize to my friend," he answered without looking back.

Andi crossed her arms and then bit her lip as she watched Mark slink away toward the darkening shoreline of the lake. She could feel eyes on her and turned suddenly to glare at Dana.

"I wish all of you would just lighten up a bit," she snapped. "I was just having a little bit of fun. There's no harm in any of it."

"They've been friends since the third grade," Dana replied. "What you just did isn't cool and it isn't funny."

Andi rolled her eyes and waved her hand toward Dana dismissively. "Whatever," she said. "Let me have one," she then added, holding out her palm.

Dana looked around uncomfortably. "What? You want one right now?" she asked, astonished.

Andi opened and closed her fingers in her palm rapidly. "Come on, give me one," she demanded.

Dana winced and looked around to make sure no one was watching.

"No one cares, Dana," Andi snapped, clearly annoyed.

"Really?" Dana clapped back. "I bet Mark would care." She reluctantly reached into her back pocket and retrieved a pack of Jupiter cigarettes. Quickly, she slid one from the carton and handed it to Andi.

"Seriously? You're not going to smoke one with me?" she asked as she snatched the cigarette.

"Not right now, no," Dana answered.

Andi retrieved a lighter from her jean shorts pocket. Dana wondered if it would actually work since it had been under water not that long ago. Andi flicked it with her thumb, and it sparked to life. She lit the cigarette and took a long drag. "God, I wish you'd stop being so uptight," she muttered as she blew a cloud of smoke from her lips. "And for the record, I don't care what Mark thinks."

Dana sighed. "Then why are you with him?" she asked.

Andi smiled and flicked some ash off onto the ground. "You really want to know?" she asked.

Dana nodded.

"Okay," she answered, moving closer to her. "I found out that Brian is a virgin. I've got a bet going with Susan Hoffman that I can change that by the end of the summer."

Dana rolled her eyes. "Oh my god," she said, making no attempt to hide her distaste. "So, you're just using him for a stupid bet?"

Andi took another pull from the cigarette and in the increasing darkness the cherry glowed bright red. She considered the question and eventually shrugged, then said, "Well, I mean he is one of the most sought-after boys in school," she said. "I kinda wanted to stay with him but now I'm having second thoughts."

"What? Why, exactly?" Dana asked incredulously. "Mark is a great guy and one of the most popular boys in school."

"Yeah, but I'm starting to think he's a bit of a wimp," she said. "I mean I thought for sure when he found out that Brian saw my boobs before he did that it would–

"Stop it," Dana said, holding up her hand. "I don't want to hear any more of this."

Andi laughed. "Dana, stop trying to act like you're such a good girl all the time," she said. "You're no angel!"

The words stung because Dana knew they were true, but they didn't stop her. She walked away feeling shameful.

***

By the time Mark had caught up to Brian, he was holding a hatchet. When he saw it, he stopped abruptly and held up his hands.

"Geez, I knew you were pissed but I had no idea it was that bad," he said, smiling.

Brian tossed the hatchet, flipping it once in the air before catching it by the handle. "Don't tempt me," he replied coldly. "I'm going to cut some wood so we can have a fire later."

"Hey, that's a good idea," Mark said, following him into the woods.

"You probably won't think that when I throw your girlfriend into the fire," Brian scoffed.

"Dang man, that's a bit harsh, isn't it?"

Brian said nothing. He had walked about twenty feet when he came upon a fallen tree with plenty of branches sprouting in all directions from its trunk. He immediately began hacking away at one, eventually freeing it and then tossing it back to Mark.

"Look, I'm sorry, man," Mark said as he caught it. "Andi told me she played a prank on you. She was just having some fun. I should've believed you."

"Yeah," Brian grunted as he cut another limb. "You should have. Why the heck would I try to take your girl like that?"

"You're right, and I know how you feel about Dana," he conceded. "I should've thought about that."

"Why are you even with her, Mark?"

He chuckled at the question. "Dude, you've seen her, right?"

Brian scowled at him. "Yeah, I saw more of her than I wanted to today," he grumbled.

That made Mark wince. "Ugh, yeah, again, sorry," he said. "But you have to admit, she's a pretty girl."

"Yeah, she's pretty," Brian admitted. "On the outside anyway."

"Damn man, you really can't stand her, can you?"

Brian stopped his work on the dead tree for a moment and turned to face Mark. "Nope, I can't," he said flatly. "But I'm going to tolerate her tonight. You know why?"

Mark stared at him, blinking.

"I've already lied to my aunt and uncle to be here," he began, pointing the hatchet toward Mark. "If they find out I dragged Barry out here, I'm toast. I did this because it's my best chance to have any shot with Dana. If I have to deal with the Wicked Witch of the West for a little while to get the girl of my dreams, then so be it."

Mark smiled and nodded. He approached Brian and put a hand on his shoulder. "I can respect that man," he said. "And I promise I'm gonna do whatever I can to help you out."

Barry rolled his eyes and returned his attention to the dead tree. "If you really want to help me," he said. "Keep your girlfriend out of my way."

"That's a deal," Mark replied as he leaned over to pick up another branch.

Brian suddenly turned to him again, as if something else had suddenly occurred to him. "And you know what else you could've done to help me out, buddy?" he asked, placing special emphasis on the word *buddy*.

Mark's eyebrows raised. "Crap, what did I do?" he asked, genuinely concerned.

"I knew you were bringing Carl, and Nicole is cool, but you could've kept George Valentine away from here," he said, glaring at him.

Mark's expression turned cloudy. He shook his head. "I don't understand," he muttered, confused. "What's wrong with George?"

Brian closed his eyes and pinched the bridge of his nose. "Seriously, Mark?" he asked, clearly growing more agitated. "He's got his eyes on Dana too. You knew that."

Mark slapped a hand to his forehead. "Dammit," he groaned. "I completely forgot that you told me that."

"Of course you did," Brian said, shaking his head.

"Man, after I got my haircut, I ran into the grocery store just to pick up some eats for tonight. They were literally clocking out for the day and George just asked me what I was up to. Without thinking, I spilled the beans on the party to them and next thing you know, they're wanting to know if they can tag along. Crap dude, I'm really sorry!"

Brian sighed. "It's fine," he said, now just eager to move on. "If I can deal with Andi, I guess I can deal with George."

"You never know," Mark said with a goofy grin. "Mossback may show up and take him out for you."

Brian was about to tell Mark that as much as he didn't want George there, he didn't have anything personally against him and wished him no harm. Before he could get the words out, their conversation was interrupted by a blood curdling scream that echoed through the forest, seemingly originating from the campground. Brian knew immediately who it was; it was Dana.

CHAPTER SEVEN

Brian and Mark sprinted back up the hill and didn't stop running until they reached the Dining Hall. There, they found Dana sitting on the ground and crying. Andi was standing beside her, and she'd placed a hand on her shoulder, apparently trying to comfort her.

"What the heck happened?" Mark asked, as he skidded to a stop in the loose gravel.

"Dana, are you okay?" Brian asked, now panting and full of adrenaline.

Dana looked up at both of them, her eyes glistening with moisture. "I saw something," she muttered with a slight quake in her voice.

Brian peered over at Andi and narrowed his eyes. "What did you do?" he asked curtly.

Andi's mouth dropped open, and she immediately put her hands on her hips. "What did I do?" she shot back. "The only thing I did was come running to check on her just like the two of you just did."

"What did you see?" Brian asked, still keeping an accusatory gaze on Andi.

She shook her head and wiped her eyes. "You're not going to believe me," she said. "I'm not even sure if I believe it."

"Just take your time and tell us what you saw," Brian urged, finally shifting his eyes to meet hers.

She held out a hand and he took it, pulling her back to her feet. She stood close to him, and he resisted the strong temptation he felt to put an arm around her.

"All three of you left me here alone so I thought I'd walk over to the playground and sit down on the merry-go-round," she began, her voice now becoming steadier again. "I was just going to sit there and wait for someone to come back. I'd just sat down when I heard what sounded like heavy breathing somewhere behind me. I looked back toward the woods, but of course it was too dark for me to see anything."

"Did it sound like it was close to you?" Mark asked. "Deer can make some weird sounds sometimes."

She shook her head. "I know this wasn't a deer because I saw it," she said. "It sounded like it was no more than fifty feet away from me. I stood up and approached the woods, just trying to get a better look. Suddenly I saw movement. Something big moved between the front row of trees. It moved away from me, but it wasn't moving very fast, and it didn't seem like it had any fear at all toward me."

"What did it look like?" Brian asked, now quite intrigued.

Dana closed her eyes and tried to replay the image back in her head. "I couldn't make out any features. It was just too dark," she said. "I just know it was large, and it walked on two feet. It had to be at least seven feet tall, and it was heavy, I could hear every step it made when it moved."

"So, it was a person?" Andi asked. She looked around in all directions when she asked the question as if she were expecting someone to pop out of the forest at any moment.

Dana bit her lip as she contemplated the question. "I'm not sure," she said after thinking for a minute. "I know that sounds crazy, but I'm just not sure what I saw."

Suddenly the conversation Brian had with Uncle Chuck earlier that afternoon began replaying in his mind. At the time, all talk about Native

American shamanism sounded like nothing more but an attempt to scare him into doing what he was told. Uncle Chuck had even admitted as much.

"It doesn't sound crazy," Brian said. "You saw what you saw."

"But what was it?" she asked, her eyes pleading for some sort of logical explanation.

"Isn't it obvious?" Andi asked. "Sounds to me like Mossback is back to celebrate the anniversary of the massacre he did twenty-five years ago." There was a hint of a smirk on her face. She was clearly skeptical.

Brian tried to work out in his head how Andi could've pulled off a prank like this. He couldn't think of a way that her small frame could've dressed up and pretended to be a seven-foot-tall monster. And Mark had of course been with him, so it wasn't him either, he thought.

"Could it have been George, or Carl playing a trick on you?" Brian asked, stepping past her to get a better look into the forest. He squinted, looking for any sign of movement.

She followed him, feeling safer near him. "I doubt that" she said. "This thing was big."

"Carl is pretty big," Mark chimed in. "And he's a jokester so I wouldn't put it past him."

Brian huffed. "It better not be," he said. "I've had enough of the pranks," he grumbled, shooting a hard look at Andi. There was no denying the smirk now.

"Well, I think I'd rather find out it was him instead of some strange weirdo stalking us in the woods tonight," Mark countered.

Brian couldn't deny the validity of his point when he thought about it.

"I don't know," Dana said sharply, her voice now the strongest it had been since she'd screamed. "Maybe my eyes were just playing tricks on me."

"I suppose it's a possibility we can't fully rule out," Brian said, looking carefully at her. "But now I can't help but worry about Barry. He and Carl need to hurry back."

"They'll be back any minute now," Mark said. "Until I see or hear anything for myself, I'm just going to chalk this up to Dana's imagination running wild. Let's go get our wood and get a fire going. That'll calm everyone down."

Dana moved even closer to Brian and now it was obvious that she was seeking comfort from him. Slowly, and clumsily, he raised his arm and gently put it around her, cupping his hand around her shoulder. There was a tiny part of him that began to wonder if there wasn't some truth to what Uncle Chuck had warned him about regarding the creature known as Mossback. An even larger part of him, however, refused to put very much stock into the story. Monsters are not real, he told himself. The moment he was having with Dana was in fact very real though and he didn't want it to end any time soon.

"Come on," he told her. "Stay with us while we go collect firewood. If Mossback is out there, he wouldn't dare come after all of us at once." He flashed her a reassuring smile and she smiled back.

"Lead the way," she said.

Brian did, and she and Mark immediately followed.

"Wait for me," Andi said, briskly chasing after them.

Brian thought he picked up the slightest tinge of fear in Andi's voice. After all she'd done to him that night, for some reason that tiny crack in the tough girl persona she'd been carrying scared him. Ultimately, if Andi was scared then it meant she truly had nothing to do with what Dana had experienced. This was troubling considering the fact that he really did not believe Dana's eyes had deceived her. It now seemed someone—or something, truly was out there.

***

"Did you hear a scream?" Nicole Phillips asked.

George Valentine did in fact hear a scream off in the distance, but he wasn't worried about it. "Andi is probably playing around," he said. "She's always trying to scare people and stir up some trouble. I couldn't stand it when we were dating and it's one of the reasons why we broke up. She needs to grow up. Anyway, you're avoiding my question. Are you going to do this or not?"

Nicole shifted her weight from one foot to the other and she stared up at the water tower that loomed large overhead.

"Are you sure this is safe?"

"Are you kidding me?" George replied as he reached out and tugged on the ladder. "This thing has been here for at least a hundred years. It ain't going anywhere."

Nicole placed her hands on her hips and shook her head skeptically. "I don't know," she said. "I think the fact that this thing is a hundred years old is exactly why I'm worried about it being unsafe."

George ignored her and decided he'd just start climbing. He'd spent the past ten minutes trying to convince her to climb the old tower with him. It was a place that held fond memories for him. He could remember his dad taking him to see it when he was ten years old and watching his dad climb it. He had been forbidden to follow and was forced to just watch from the ground. When his dad reached the top, he could remember hearing the excitement in his voice and the description he gave of the landscape surrounding them. He'd sworn that day that he'd eventually return and climb it for himself so he could experience the same view his dad had seen. The opportunity had finally presented itself.

"Come on," he said, peering back at her.

Nicole smacked her gum and blew a bubble as she considered it. She was wearing black shorts and a pink sweatshirt that sported teal sleeves. Her long black hair was pulled back into a ponytail. She was only fifteen, two years younger than George. They couldn't be more different and the only reason they'd gotten to know each other was because they both worked together at the grocery store. Though they'd become close friends, in her view their relationship was very similar to that of a brother and sister. George often drove her home after work. On the days when her shift ended before his, he'd give her whatever quarters he had in his pocket so she could go and play *Pac-Man* at the arcade across the street until he was finished. He'd gotten about halfway up the ladder when Nicole finally mustered up the courage to grab onto the first rung.

"Okay," she said nervously. "I'm coming up."

"Just one step at a time," George said, looking down at her. "Take your time and I'll see you at the top."

The water tower was almost entirely made of wood. George wouldn't admit it to Nicole, but he was actually surprised at how good the condition of the wood was considering its age. The tower had been built well, and it was solid, a testament to the quality of the work and materials that was prominent long ago. He was glad that Nicole was with him because if he was really honest with himself, he was still trying to figure out how he truly felt about her. Nicole was cute and only a couple of years younger than him. He knew it wouldn't be long before the other guys would begin to notice her and by then it could be too late if he wanted to pursue anything. But ultimately did he really want her to be his girlfriend? Again, if he were honest with himself that answer was currently 'no'. The girl that he really wanted right now was Dana Berkley, but he didn't know if he had a real shot with her or not because his ex-girlfriend, Andi Parker, was her closest friend. Who knew what sort of trash Andi had told her about him, he thought. When he found out from his friend Mark that Dana was going to be at Camp Beaver Brook that very night, he knew it was his chance to talk to her and feel things out.

"You, okay?" he asked, pausing to check on Nicole.

"I'm good," she said, gesturing back at him with a thumbs up.

He heard her blow another bubble and the pop that followed. George climbed several more rungs when he finally reached the square platform on which the cylindrical tank with the metal cone roof rested on. He carefully took a few steps on the wooden planks to make sure they were still solid and strong enough to support his weight. He knew there were massive support beams underneath that carried the brunt of the tank's weight but in the waning light it was nearly impossible to tell where they were. While he waited for Nicole to catch up, he dusted off his jeans and then, for the very first time, took a look at the surrounding landscape. Off to the west he could see the orange glow of the sun as it began to dip down below the horizon. There was just enough light for him to make out some of the buildings and houses in Darkwood, several miles away. He could easily see the steeple of the First Baptist Church on Main Street. To the north he caught a glimpse of the Chester River that winded through the entire length of the county. To the east he could plainly see the cabins and other structures that made up Camp Beaver Brook along with the large lake next to it. He could see four people walking, two girls and two boys. He squinted and soon deduced that it was Dana, Andi, Mark and Brian Lancaster, a boy he didn't know that well. All he really knew about Brian was that he was a great varsity basketball player and a good friend of Mark's. He also noticed that Brian had his arm around Dana. This was totally unexpected, and he was taken aback. He wondered if they were a couple.

"Oh my god, I can't believe I did this," Nicole said suddenly, as her head appeared over the edge of the platform.

George hurried over to her and knelt down, offering his hand to her. She took it and he pulled her up.

"Are you afraid of heights?" he asked her.

She glared at him. "You're asking me that now?"

"Well, I wasn't trying to give you any reason to not follow me up here," he confessed. "I didn't want you to miss out on this view."

"Well for the record, I'm not afraid of heights," she replied as she stood up. When she looked around, her mouth dropped open. "Wow, this is so cool!"

"I know, right?"

They stood there for a few minutes and didn't move until the sun had finally completely disappeared and the stars began to pepper the darkened sky.

"Great. What a safe place to be in total darkness," she said sarcastically upon realizing the light was gone.

"It's not that bad," he answered assuringly. "Your eyes will adjust. And besides," he added, shoving a hand into his pocket. He retrieved a small black object. She heard the click of a button and suddenly a bright light illuminated their vicinity. "I brought a flashlight."

She nodded her approval. "Okay, now I feel like I have a chance of getting down without dying."

"You're not gonna die," George said. "And you're not going back down yet either."

She looked around, confused. "Okay, where exactly am I going then?"

"Follow me," he said, turning away from her.

"Wait up," she snapped, reaching out to grab his shirt tail. He was wearing an old Darkwood High School baseball t-shirt with the sleeves torn off. "Where are you going?"

"Don't you want to see what's on the other side?" he asked, unwilling to let her slow him down.

"Couldn't we just do that from the ground?"

"Yeah, but where's the fun in that?" he replied.

They made their way around the wooden shell of the tank, careful to stay against it as much as possible because there was no railing to keep them from falling over the other side. George kept the beam of light steadily ahead of him and his eyes searched for any potential hazard. He was again amazed at how good the condition of the water tower actually was.

"Do you think it still has water in it?" Nicole asked, her hand still tightly gripping his shirt.

"I'm pretty sure it doesn't," he answered.

She scowled at him. "And just how would you know that?"

"Do you really think this thing could support that much weight for so many years without collapsing by now? Now stay close to the side, we're almost to the back," he said.

Nicole did as he had instructed and practically dragged her shoulder along the wood as they advanced. Suddenly, with no warning at all, George fell over. His shirt jerked free from her hand, and he was completely gone from view. She heard him yelp and at first could not tell if he was just startled or hurt. For a moment, she had trouble processing what had actually occurred and saw no signs of the flashlight.

"Dang, I wasn't expecting that!" she heard him say as the beam of light began to dance around in front of her again. "Look at this!"

His head was poking out from inside the tank. Nicole took another step forward and realized there was an enormous hole in the side of it. It seemed George had unexpectedly fallen over and into the void.

"I guess you were right about there being no water inside," she said, as he helped her in.

George shone the flashlight around the interior of the tank. A few bats fluttered near the top, startling them both. For the most part, the tank was empty and completely dry. There were, however, a few curious things that immediately caught their attention.

"Is that...hay?" Nicole asked, squinting.

George nodded and moved closer allowing the light to lead him. "Yep, that's a little weird," he said. "Maybe an animal was using this as a den or something."

The hay was piled high and the center of it was mashed inward as if something heavy had been lying in it. There was also an old dirty blanket that looked like the spread from a twin sized bed. A few feet away from the hay lay a pile of bones. Most of the bones were tiny. Probably birds, George thought. There was a tattered Camp Beaver Brook t-shirt on the floor that was heavily stained. George shined the light on the shirt and thought the stains resembled blood.

"Is that what I think it is?" Nicole muttered, apparently thinking the same thing.

"Nah, I doubt it," George said, doing his best to sound confident though he wasn't sure if he was doing it for Nicole's benefit or his own.

He moved the light further across the floor and spotted old soda cans and a few interesting-looking bowls. George kept the light focused on the bowls and walked over to them to see if there were any remnants of food there.

"What are those?" Nicole asked. "Those aren't bowls. Oh my god, George, is that hair?"

George stopped dead in his tracks when he noticed it. Nicole was right, they did not appear to actually be bowls at all. There seemed to be strands of hair attached to some of them.

"Umm, George what the heck are those?" Nicole asked, now sounding slightly panicked.

He felt a wave of nausea suddenly wash over him and a cold sweat formed on his forehead. He backed away. "I think we need to leave," he said softly.

"Tell me what those are," she persisted, now pointing. "I want to know if I'm crazy or–"

"Skulls," George interrupted. "I think those are the tops of skulls."

Chapter Eight

"Do you think the lake has any fish in it?" Barry asked as they spotted Mark's white Ford Thunderbird.

"Man, I hope so," Carl said. "If we could catch a few catfish we're gonna be eating real good tonight!"

The sun was completely gone now but there was a purple hue in the western sky that provided just enough light for them to still be able to see.

"How are we going to see our way back?" Barry asked as he gazed upward at the first smattering of stars that appeared.

"Don't worry, I've got it covered," Carl said. He used the key to open the trunk, reached inside and brought out a flashlight. He held it up proudly and turned it on. There was a low fog rolling overhead and the beam from the flashlight became easily visible.

"Cool!" Barry said excitedly. "It's like a lightsaber!"

When Carl noticed it, he quickly placed both hands around the light, holding it like a sword. "Barry," he said, his voice very deep. "I am your father."

Barry laughed. He liked Carl a lot. He didn't treat him so much like a little kid the way Brian and his other friends did.

"Here," Carl said, handing over a fishing pole he'd retrieved from the trunk. "Hold this."

Barry took it and looked on as Carl then pulled out a tackle box and a six pack of beer. "We should've grabbed some ice," he said ruefully, shutting the trunk. "Come on kid, let's head back."

Carl led them back toward the trail when suddenly they heard a sound behind them that immediately brought them to a halt.

"What was that?" Barry asked.

Carl shrugged. "Sounded like someone walking under those trees," he said, shining the light toward the woods on the other side of the car.

"Who would be out there?"

"I think I know who," Carl replied with a sly grin. "Your brother is probably trying to get some revenge on me for scaring him earlier."

Barry nodded. "So, what are you going to do?" he asked.

Carl turned off the flashlight and handed it over to Barry. "I think I saw him moving under that big oak tree," he said. "Keep this light off and stay out of sight. I'm going to go mess with Brian and then we'll all head back together."

"Okay, get him good," Barry said, smiling mischievously.

Carl winked at him and then moved quickly to the Thunderbird again. He crouched down behind it and then slowly peered over the hood, watching for any sign of movement again. He saw nothing but definitely heard the sound of footsteps on the forest floor again in the same area where he'd seen someone moving. He moved to the rear of the car and then made a beeline for a patch of huckleberry bushes. Once there he moved deeper into the woods, doing his best to stay within the darkest shadows to avoid being seen. Carl moved methodically, pausing every few seconds behind a tree, and then peering around the trunk like a predator stalking its prey. He spotted another glimpse of a moving shadow and then darted closer, keeping his feet light on the ground. Carl smiled as he drew even closer and prepared to sprint toward Brian so he could tackle him to the ground. If everything went right, Brian would be so caught so off guard he'd experience the fright of his life. The scare he'd received earlier would pale in comparison. Again, Carl spotted movement. The time had finally arrived. He took off like he'd just left the line of scrimmage in a football game. In a way, this was practice, he thought. It was common for him to find a way to associate almost everything he did with football. He scanned the environment ahead of him for movement again. At first, he saw nothing, but then, unexpectedly, something massive stepped in front of him. Carl tried to stop, and when he did, his feet slid out from under him. He fell on his back, his head striking the ground hard. Carl blinked twice, but everything in his vision was dark and blurry. The silhouette of Brian loomed over him.

Or was it, Brian?

Suddenly, without warning, the silhouette dipped down at him. He felt a cold, wet hand close around his throat. The next thing he knew, Carl was being lifted off the ground. He reached for the hand on his throat. The grip was incredibly strong and despite his best efforts, he couldn't pull himself free. The hand tightened and Carl began to panic as he realized his airway had been completely closed off. He kicked at the person's belly but to his horror, it seemed to make absolutely no difference. Carl tried to scream, but he couldn't get a single sound out, nor could he take a breath. Now he could tell he was moving. His attacker was actually walking with him held out in its outstretched hand as if he were nothing more than a mere doll. Carl continued to thrash wildly, kicking his legs forward with all his might, doing anything and everything he could think of to turn the odds in his favor. Then, he felt the searing pain. Something had pierced through his back, tearing flesh and breaking bone as it moved through his body. Suddenly, the thing tearing through his body erupted from his chest and it was at that moment Carl realized he'd been impaled onto a jagged branch that jutted out from the very oak tree he'd been watching minutes earlier.

Finally, the grip on his throat was released. Carl allowed his head to flop forward, and he could plainly see the branch protruding from his chest, blood dripping from the end of it. More blood poured down the front of his body and onto his jogging pants, soaking them to the point that they felt ridiculously heavy on his legs. His body began to get cold. Soon the terrible pain in his abdomen began to fade and so did everything around him. Everything soon became enveloped in permanent, cold darkness.

***

Barry could hear movement, but something sounded sickeningly off. What he'd expected to hear was a frightened yelp from Brian followed by hearty laughing. He'd expected to then see his brother and Carl step out of the shadowed blackness of the forest, at which point he could turn on his flashlight to greet them. Barry unfortunately heard none of that. Instead, he remained motionless, straining his ears to make out anything at all to clue him in on what was happening. He'd considered calling Carl's name out, but feared if he did it would ruin the whole prank that he was trying to pull off. The last thing Barry wanted to do was make Carl think he was a big scaredy cat. So he continued to wait.

The waiting went on for several minutes and the silence became so heavy Barry swore he literally felt it pressing down on him. Finally, he could take it no more, so he stood and reluctantly called out Carl's name.

"Carl," he said in a flat tone. He'd resisted yelling, because he didn't want to come across as frightened.

When there was no reply, he called his name out again, this time a bit louder. "Carl."

Just when he thought he'd get no response again, he did in fact hear something. But what he heard was not at all what he expected. It was breathing. Each breath was deep and steady, making it seem as though whoever was breathing was quite large.

"Hello?" he said meekly. "Is anyone out there?"

No one replied to him, but the sound of heavy footsteps began. Whoever, or whatever, was breathing so heavily in the woods was now clearly moving toward him. Barry contemplated turning on the flashlight to illuminate whoever was approaching but the thought was quickly stamped out by the wave of guttural fear that began to overcome him. Without considering the matter any further, Barry allowed his survival instincts to take control. He dropped the fishing pole beside the tackle box and took off running.

Chapter Nine

Chuck and Sara had to park on the road outside of the cemetery. Darkness had fallen but the site was well lit by multiple utility lights spread throughout the rows of graves. The memorial had drawn a much larger crowd than they'd expected.

"It's hard to believe that after twenty-five years the people in this community still feel so connected by this," Sara said as she swung open her door and stepped out. She walked to the front of the car, her high heels wobbling in the gravel.

Chuck met her and offered an arm to steady her. "It was multiple murders which affected multiple families. Some of these families are pretty big. It wouldn't surprise me at all if all these people were somehow related to one of the victims."

She shot him with a curious look. "You talk about them like we didn't know them," she said. "They were our friends."

He sighed and nodded. "I know, you're right," he said. "It was just so long ago."

They entered through the gates and strode toward the crowd near the southeast corner of the property. When they reached them, everyone turned and looked at them as if they were celebrities, or some important political figures. Chuck and Sara smiled as politely as they could, but being known for surviving the most horrific event in Darkwood's history wasn't something they'd gotten used to.

"Here we go again," he said, through clenched teeth.

"Be polite," Sara said sternly.

The crowd moved aside, and people motioned for them to head toward the front of the assembly. Chuck considered a polite refusal but thought better of it. It was better to give them what they wanted, and whether he liked it or not, he and Sara were as much a part of the memorial as the four identical tombstones they were now being ushered toward. When they finally did reach the front of the crowd they were met by a man of average height with balding red hair and a mustache. He was wearing a black suit that was a stark contrast to his overly white skin tone. Beside him was Sheriff Howard Turner who eyed both of them anxiously. It was as if he'd been waiting for them specifically, Chuck thought.

"Mr. and Mrs. Lancaster," the redheaded man said, offering a hand. "Thank you for attending this memorial, I know it means a great deal to the families of those that were lost."

Sara looked over her shoulder uncomfortably. "If our being here gives anyone even an ounce of comfort, then I'm glad we came too," she said. "It's good to see you, Pastor David."

"You as well," David replied. He leaned in close. "Please don't run off when the service is over. Sheriff Turner needed to speak with both of you."

Chuck and Sara glanced at each other briefly but nodded. "Sure thing," Chuck said.

David pulled away, glanced at his watch and realized it was time to begin.

"Everyone, I just want to start by saying how wonderful it is to see you all here," he said, his voice now booming to the volume it was normally at on Sunday mornings.

"Tonight, we remember the precious souls that were lost so tragically twenty-five years ago on this very night. I'll start by naming each one of your loved ones and we'll observe a moment of silence for each. Use that moment however you wish but for those of you that knew them, I strongly encourage you to focus on the good memories that were shared."

Chuck took a breath and braced himself to hear the names.

"Julie Davis," David began. As promised, there was a moment of silence and soon sobs could be heard sporadically throughout the assembly. David then continued on naming Earl Holly, James Dearing, and of course, Jake Simpson.

Chuck and Sara's memories of Jake were of course unpleasant, but it wasn't lost on them that he too was someone's child, sibling, and friend. People cried and grieved for his death just as they did the other three.

"These four young people were taken from us in a cruel and unfair fashion," David continued. "And I sense many of you still feel like there is unfinished business here. After all, the monster that was responsible for taking their lives was never apprehended. I'd be remiss if I didn't mention the belief that some have regarding the possibility that the killer wasn't a person at all, but a creature. Something not of this earth."

Chuck peered over at Sara in disbelief. "Is he really going there?" he whispered.

Her eyes widened in shock, and she shook her head with disgust.

"Well, I'm here to tell you that whether you believe the killer was a man or a creature of the night, ultimately, they do not have the final say. Ladies and gentlemen, our loved ones may have been taken from us on the fateful night in 1958 but their memories live on today in 1983."

The crowd perked up a moment and there were a few somber affirmations that could be heard.

"Furthermore," David went on. "On this very night they stand by the throne of God almighty and are as healthy and happy as they can possibly be. Far better off than they could ever be on this wicked purgatory of a planet we now stand upon."

More affirmations. It was a nice sentiment, Chuck thought, but it didn't make him feel better. The fact remained that his friends were taken by someone...brutally. And it wasn't lost on him that had the killer been given the chance, he and Sara's tombstones could've easily been in the cemetery as well. What happened was tragic and barbaric. The person–or creature–responsible had never been brought to justice and that bothered him to no end.

Pastor David continued on with the service by reading passages from the Bible as well as offering members of the family a chance to speak if they wanted to. Only one woman chose to speak, an elderly lady, the mother of Julie Davis. She wept as she discussed the hopes and dreams, she'd had for Julie. She'd encouraged her to follow her dream of becoming a teacher and had no doubts she would have been masterful at it. Before Sara knew it, she found herself crying as she remembered her friend from so long ago.

When the service finally ended, people began to file away and soon there was only Pastor David and Sheriff Turner standing in front of Chuck and Sara.

"Again, I thank you for coming to this," David said, shaking both their hands. "The people of Darkwood appreciate it more than you know. They say time heals all wounds, but I don't know if it's necessarily the case here."

Chuck shrugged. "I'd be lying if I told you I understand what you mean, because I don't," he said. "We came here tonight because we truly wanted to pay our respects to our old friends. If by doing that, it somehow helps this community, then so be it."

"The two of you are survivors!" David said, a bit too enthusiastically, Chuck thought. "You're a beacon of hope for the family members that were left behind. Again, thank you so much for attending."

"Thanks, pastor," Sara said as he walked away.

Sheriff Turner stepped closer with his hands in his pockets as he watched David get into his car. "I've always thought that fella was a little odd," he confessed with a mischievous grin.

Chuck smiled and let out a relieved breath. "Thank god I'm not the only one that was thinking it," he said.

"He definitely seems a little infatuated by the two of you. Do you attend his church?"

Sara chuckled. "Of course not, we're Methodists," she said flatly.

"I think the guy means well, but I hope the next time they do one of these memorials they get someone else to lead it," Turner said.

"Me too," Chuck replied. "He said you had something you needed to tell us?"

Sheriff Turner's eyes widened, and he adjusted his cowboy hat. "Yeah, I do have something I need to share with you," he said. "But I'm kinda hungry. Can I buy the two of you some dinner?"

Chuck looked at Sara about the time she looked at him. "Sheriff, that's very kind, but it's not necessary," he said.

Turner held up his hands. "I insist," he shot back. "Follow me. There's a diner I like only a couple of blocks away."

The sheriff turned and began walking toward his police cruiser without another word.

"Why is everyone being weird tonight?" Sara asked, a bit perplexed.

"I don't know. But if we want to find out what he's got to tell us, I suppose we better follow him," Chuck said.

Chapter Ten

"They sure are taking their sweet time," Andi said as she felt her stomach growl. "I hope you brought some other snacks," she added, peering over at Mark. "If all we've got to depend on is Carl catching a few fish, I'm not that hopeful."

Mark scowled as he sat down beside her. They, along with Dana and Brian, were seated on a large log next to the lake. A campfire crackled in front of them. "Carl isn't a bad fisherman," he said. "What are you talking about?"

"We don't even know if there are any fish in this lake," Andi said, gesturing toward the body of water as if it were nothing more than a puddle on the street.

"I think there are some," Brian said, gazing at the lake. The stars reflected onto its eerily smooth surface.

"Really, how do you know?" Dana asked, genuinely curious.

He eyed her carefully and then glanced at Andi. "Well, I mean, I was in the water earlier," he quipped. "Maybe if Andi wasn't so preoccupied with being a jerk, she'd have noticed them like I did."

Andi shot him a cold look and raised her chin dismissively, returning her attention to Mark. "So did you bring any snacks or not?"

Mark patted her leg. "Of course I did, babe," he said. "And some booze too. Do you want me to go and get them?"

She nodded and smiled prettily at him. He rose to his feet, but before he could leave, he noticed George and Nicole appear in the clearing between the Dining Hall and playground on top of the hill. "Well, look who finally decided to show up," he said, pointing.

The other three turned and watched as George and Nicole jogged down the hill to where they were. Brian had been dreading George's arrival but did his best to hide it.

"You're not going to believe what we just found," Nicole said, her eyes wide with excitement.

"Oh my god, I'm afraid to ask," Dana replied, standing.

"Human skulls!" Nicole said. "Can you believe that? Human skulls!"

"Wait, are you serious?" Brian asked, suddenly no longer very concerned about George's presence.

Nicole nodded enthusiastically.

"Well, hold on," George said, his voice calm and steady. "We think that's what they were, we're not totally certain."

"How can you not be certain?" Andi asked. "Do you not know what a human skull looks like?"

"Well yeah, but it looked like it was only the top part of the skull," George replied. "It was like someone had cut off the tops of several heads. It was really weird."

"Where did you find them?" Brian asked, stunned at the news.

"They were in the old water tower in the woods," George explained.

"Yeah, we climbed it," Nicole chimed in, still barely able to contain her excitement. "And when we got up there, we found out someone had been living in it!"

"Living in it?" Mark asked, directing his attention to George for clarification.

George nodded. "I suppose it could be some kind of animal though," he said with a shrug.

Nicole shook her head, blew a bubble, then said, "No, I'm sure it's not an animal that's been living there. A person had been there, I just know it."

Suddenly they all heard another commotion from up the hill near the entrance to the trail. A beam from a flashlight danced around wildly as someone ran toward them.

"Brian!" Barry called out sharply when he reached them.

Brian and the others had to hold their hands up to shield their eyes from the blinding light.

"Barry, turn the light off!" Andi hissed.

"What's wrong?" Brian asked, immediately snatching the flashlight away and turning it off.

Barry leaned forward, panting, and placed his hands on his knees. "Something...happened...to Carl," he muttered.

Brian and Mark looked at each other.

"What happened to him?" Dana asked. "Is he okay?"

"I...don't know," he replied, shaking his head. "He went into the woods, and he didn't come out."

"Wait, why did he leave you?" Brian asked, trying to gather all the facts so he could understand.

Barry's breathing finally returned to normal, and he stood up straight. "He heard someone in the woods, so he went to check it out," he said. "He thought it was you trying to get him back for scaring you earlier."

"Well did he scream or make any sound at all?" George asked.

Barry shook his head. "No, he just never came out."

Mark laughed. "Then I'm sure he's still out there," he said. "Carl's messing with you, kid."

Barry shook his head again. "No, someone else was there, I could hear them!"

"See, I told you," Nicole said, her expression now smug. "A person has been living in that water tower; probably the same person that just got Carl."

"Okay, Nicole," George said, holding up his hand. "That's enough, you're just speculating at this point."

Brian could see the panic and fear in his younger brother's face. "Okay, I think maybe we should go look for Carl," he said, glancing up the hill.

"No," Barry said, pleading and grabbing his brother's arm. "Don't go back up there."

"At this point I don't think we have a choice," Mark said, walking away. "Because you didn't even bring the fishing pole and tackle back with you."

"Guys, hang on a minute," George said. "Did you forget about what Nicole, and I just told you about what we found at the water tower?"

"No, I plainly remember you saying you found a den for what may or may not have been a person in the water tower," Mark shot back. "Oh, and you found what may or may not have been pieces of human skulls. Is that about, right?"

"Don't go up there by yourself," George said. "I'm telling you I don't feel so good about this."

Mark stared at him and smirked. "Wait, are you really telling me you're too scared to go back up there with me?" he asked, amused. "Five seconds ago, you were telling Nicole to not speculate and now you're literally doing the same thing."

George looked away and sighed.

"What about you, Brian?" he asked.

Brian clenched his jaw and shook his head, now rethinking this.

Mark's jaw dropped and he began to laugh. "Wow, I can't believe this! You two are actually scared!"

"I'll go with you babe," Andi said, hooking her arm around his.

Mark smiled and kissed her on the cheek. "Okay, we'll be back in a few minutes," he told them. "Don't let that fire die out!"

"Mark, be careful," Brian called after him.

He waved a hand in the air as he continued to walk away, not looking back.

Andi said, "Don't worry, Brian. I'll protect him from Mossback!"

The two of them laughed as they trudged up the hill. The others quietly watched them until they'd completely disappeared into the woods.

"They're gonna die," Nicole said nonchalantly, ending the silence.

George peered over at her in disbelief. "Not funny, Nikki," he growled.

"So, what do we do now?" Dana asked. "This night isn't at all turning out how I thought it would."

"Well, the night is still young," George answered, flashing a smile.

Dana smiled back. Brian noticed it and felt his face get hot.

"I know it's not the popular opinion," Brian said. "But do you guys think we should stay out here? Something weird is going on."

George nodded. "Yeah, if they don't come back in a few minutes with Carl, I say we get out of here."

"Don't count on them coming back in a few minutes," Dana said.

"What?" Nicole asked. "Why not?"

Dana shifted her feet uncomfortably and looked away. "I just wouldn't be surprised if they make a stop somewhere along the way," she said.

Nicole rolled her eyes. "Oh my god," she groaned. "That slut is at it again, huh?"

Brian laughed. He couldn't help it. George smiled but stopped short of laughing.

"That's not nice," Dana snapped. "She's, my friend."

Nicole looked away, smirking.

"Hey Nicole," Barry said suddenly. "How's it going?"

She eyed him curiously and smiled. "It's going good, Barry. I haven't seen you at the arcade this week. What gives?"

He smiled, seemingly thrilled she had an interest in talking back to him. "My mom and dad are out of town; I've been staying with my aunt and uncle. They live on the other side of Darkwood."

"Your aunt and uncle, huh?" she asked. "Do they know you're out here, Barry?"

Brian cleared his throat. "It doesn't matter," he said. "They trust me to look after him and that's what I'm doing."

"Well, that's sweet to hear, Brian," she replied, smacking her gum. "But if Mossback shows up, who is going to look after you?"

***

Mark led Andi clumsily along the trail in darkness. His eyes were beginning to adjust, and he was grateful that the full moon had now risen to the point that its silver light provided enough visibility to get by without a light.

"You should've grabbed the flashlight," Andi grumbled. "I feel like I'm going to trip over a rock or something at any second."

"The moon is enough," he replied. "Once we get to the clearing where my car is parked, we will be able to see really good."

Soon they came to a fork in the path. Mark stopped, and pondered his choices, clearly unsure which direction to take.

"You're lost, aren't you?" Andi asked.

He shrugged. "No, no, I'm not lost," he muttered absently. "Just confused."

She moved behind him and put her arms around his waist. "Well, we need to move," she said. "There's something I want to show you when we get to the car."

Her hands drifted to the button on his shorts.

"I think it's this way," he said, quickly moving toward the left path.

She giggled and chased after him. "You're not going to avoid me all night, are you?" she asked.

"Avoid you?" he replied nervously. "Of course not."

They walked for several minutes and just as Mark came to the realization that they had been moving much too long for them to reach the car, they came upon a large, tall structure ahead.

"What is that?" Andi asked, squinting in the dim light.

"I think that's the water tower," Mark answered.

Andi stopped walking. "Oh my god," she said, a bit startled. "The same water tower Nicole and George were talking about? The one that the homeless guy is living in?"

"Yeah, I think that's the one."

"With the skulls in it?"

Mark chuckled. "Andi, it's probably not really human skulls. George sounded really unsure about that."

"Well Nicole didn't," she rebutted.

He glanced back at her, his eyebrows raised. "Want to check it out?"

Andi almost told him no, but then she remembered the real reason why she'd wanted to come out here with Mark in the first place and recognized an opportunity. She smiled.

"What the hell," she said. "We're only gonna live once, right?"

Mark smiled back at her, and she could easily see his white teeth in the moonlight. He was clearly unbothered by any insinuations that had been made by a homeless man with a collection of skulls–or the presence of Mossback. He sprinted toward the ladder and began climbing it. She chased after him and they quickly ascended onto the platform that surrounded the base of the tank.

"They said someone has been living in this thing, but they didn't say anything about how someone would get inside it," Mark said as she made his way around the tank. "Surely there's a ladder to the top or–"

"Or what?" Andi asked as she watched him stop abruptly.

"Bingo," he said. "There's a giant hole here. Give me your hand."

She held out her hand and he took it, gently pulling her toward him. Before she even fully realized it, they were both inside the tank.

"Man, it's dark in here," Mark said. He glanced over his shoulder, back to the large hole they'd just come through. He could easily see the moon and stars sprinkled across the black sky, but it wasn't enough to illuminate the interior of the tank. Suddenly, he felt Andi grab the waistband of his denim cut-offs and pulled him toward her.

"Kiss me," she said. It was a demand, not a request.

Mark leaned forward, and his lips met hers. She fell back, pulling him with her and they clumsily fell to the ground.

"Are you sure about this?" he asked, and deep down realized the question was more for himself than for her.

"Yes," she said breathlessly. "Of course, I'm sure."

"No, I mean, do you want to do this here?" he said, looking around and wondering if they were inches away from part of someone's skull.

She pulled her shirt off, took his hand and moved it to her breast. "Do I need to say anything else?" she asked.

Mark felt an overwhelming primal urge overtake him that he'd never experienced before. Suddenly, he no longer cared about skulls, or Mossback, or anything else. He quickly pulled his football jersey off and tossed it aside. He reached for Andi's pants when suddenly he heard the sound of something moving somewhere else inside the blackness of the tank.

"What was that?" he asked.

"What was what?" she asked, a bit annoyed that he'd stopped.

"It sounded like hay moving, like someone moving around in a pile of it," he explained, his tone a bit frantic.

"You're hearing things," Andi said, trying to keep control of things. "There's no one here but me and you."

She reached down, unbuttoned his pants and then plunged her hand into his underwear. The trick worked, and Mark leaned forward to passionately kiss her again. Suddenly, the unmistakable sound of heavy footsteps began. Someone was obviously approaching them.

Andi screamed and reached for her shirt. Mark scrambled to his feet; his fists clenched.

"Who the hell is in here?" he asked, doing his best to sound intimidating.

Whoever was in the tank with them stopped walking, but they could clearly hear deep breathing. Whoever was there was just staring at them. Mark stood his ground as Andi dashed out of the tank; her shirt crumpled in her arms. She quickly reached the ladder and began climbing down it.

"Come on, Mark!" she squealed as she descended.

The response she received wasn't the one she was expecting. A guttural scream erupted from within the tank. It was a scream of pain and agony, like the sound of someone being killed. It was obviously originating from Mark. Andi could do nothing but release a panicked scream when she reached the ground. She turned to flee back to the trail from which they'd come. She'd taken no more than three steps when suddenly a large object landed on the ground in front of her. Whatever it was had seemingly been hurtled through the air, purposefully at her. It made a sickening sound when it struck the earth and despite every fiber of her being trying to convince her otherwise, Andi knew full well what it was.

"Mark?" she said aloud, desperately hoping she was wrong. Her whole body trembled now as she approached for a better look. Her heart began beating so rapidly she thought it was going to burst from her chest. To her horror, she realized that it was indeed Mark's twisted, and lifeless body sprawled before her in the moonlight; and he was missing his head.

Chapter Eleven

"What's taking them so long?" Nicole asked, glancing at the neon display on her Casio wristwatch.

"I have a pretty good idea," Dana said, annoyed.

Brian sighed and crossed his arms, looking over at her. "I know she's your friend, Dana, but Mark's my friend so I want you to level with me."

"Okay," she said, dragging the word out to suggest she was dreading the question.

"When she's done using him, she's gonna dump him, right?" he asked, matter of fact.

It was Dana's turn to cross her arms and the look she gave him wasn't a warm one. "I'm not sure what you're insinuating Brian. I'm not sure what all you've heard but for the record, when it comes to her relationships, she's been the dumpee a heck of a lot more than the dumper."

He huffed, narrowing his eyes. "Come on," he groaned.

"It's true," she shot back. "She's got an awful reputation that she's very much aware of and believe it or not, it bothers her. I've been on the phone with her at night listening to her cry when she's heard the latest rumor going around."

Brian looked away, suddenly feeling a bit guilty. It wasn't lost on him that George and Nicole hadn't made so much as a peep, and although he didn't consider either of them a real friend, he couldn't believe they didn't chime in and back him up. Barry, he noticed, was just staring at Nicole, daydreaming. God only knew what about.

"Okay," he said softly. "I'm sorry. I just don't want to see Mark done wrong. As bad as I hate to say it, he really does like her."

"And she likes him," Dana replied. She felt a tinge of shame when she said the words because she knew full well, they were not entirely true.

"I hate to interrupt," George said, looking back over his shoulder. "But did you hear that?"

"Hear what?" Brian asked. No sooner had he asked the question, he noticed it too.

"Sounds like crying," Nicole said, rising to her feet.

"It's Andi," Dana said, standing also. She began jogging up the hill.

Suddenly Andi appeared and she was crying hysterically. She made it as far as the playground before collapsing to her knees at which point she screamed.

"Andi, what's wrong?" Dana asked, dropping to her own knees and throwing her arms around her friend.

"H-he's...I can't b-believe it," she stammered through uncontrollable sobs.

Brian noticed something on her face, something dark and spattered over her cheek like freckles.

"What happened?" he asked, beginning to fear the worst. "Where is Mark?"

Andi looked over at him, the expression on her face twisted in fear and agony. "D-dead," she sputtered. "Mark's dead!"

Were the specks on her cheek blood?

Brian suddenly felt as if the entire world had dropped out from under him. He felt his knees get weak and had to reach out and grab the nearby jungle gym to keep from falling.

"Oh my god," Dana said, as she too began to cry.

"What do you mean he's dead?" George asked in disbelief. "What the hell happened to him?"

"That creep living in the water tower!" Nicole shouted, answering his question. "He got Carl and now he got Mark!"

"Andi, look at me," George said, grabbing her under the chin. "Did you and Mark go to the water tower?"

Andi nodded, tears streaming down her face. "Yes." She began to shake as another round of uncontrollable sobs began. George wrapped his arms around her, doing his best to comfort her.

"Brian, I want to go home," Barry said, his voice suddenly quaking nearly as bad as Andi's.

Brian closed his eyes and swallowed, forcing himself to remain calm as he continued to lean on the jungle gym. He felt as if he were going to be sick. "Okay," he said, finally regaining most of his composure. "We're getting out of here, right now."

He grabbed Barry by the arm and began marching toward the parking lot at the outer edge of the campground. "Everyone, follow me to my car. We need to leave now."

"Is there enough room for all of us?" George asked.

"We'll make room," Brian said, and his legs began to move faster.

No one had to be asked twice, and they all began running, not stopping until they reached the Pinto. Brian quickly slid behind the steering wheel, while Dana, Andi and Nicole squeezed into the back seat. George plopped into the passenger seat and pulled Barry onto his lap, slamming the door shut. Brian shoved the key into the ignition and turned it.

Click.

"What the hell?"

He turned it again, still nothing.

"What is it?" George asked, staring hard at him.

"Nothing's happening," he answered frantically, still turning the key back and forth. Brian pounded his fist on the steering wheel and then reached down to pop the hood. It was then he noticed it had already been opened. "Oh no," he said as the sickening realization began to hit him.

"What?" Dana asked. "What's wrong now?"

"We're gonna die," Andi said. "We're going to end up just like Mark and Carl!"

Brian ignored her as he swung open the door and quickly made his way to the front of the vehicle, lifting the hood. "George, bring the flashlight," he barked.

George appeared seconds later, flicking the light on and shining the beam into the motor bay. To their horror, the plug wires had been ripped out of the car along with the air filter and a multitude of other parts and pieces that they knew were necessary for the car to operate.

"Someone doesn't want us to leave," George said softly. "I can't believe this is happening right now."

"Everyone out of the car!" Brian called out.

He could hear them groaning and whimpering in protest, but they all exited the vehicle. Dana stepped up to them first and when she looked down at the motor she put a hand to her mouth.

"We've got to get to Mark's car," George said. The comment was directed at Brian and he suddenly felt like he'd been somehow chosen to make decisions.

He shook his head. "What good would that do, George? Carl took the keys, remember? And we have no idea where Carl is, do we?"

"Well, we could..." he paused, thinking. "We could hot wire it," he said suddenly, snapping his fingers.

"What? I don't know how to hot wire a car, do you?"

George exhaled and slumped his shoulders. "No, I guess not," he said, sounding defeated. "I was hoping you did."

Dana moved between them. "Guys, I don't think we need to stay out here," she said, her eyes darting around in all directions.

Brian nodded. "She's right," he said. "We can't stay out here. We currently don't have a way to leave. The only thing I know to do right now is get in one of those cabins and lock the door. We can work out what to do after that when we get there."

"Sounds like a plan to me," George said, turning away with the flashlight. "Follow me."

They all got behind him, single file, as he led them across the clearing, past the playground and the Dining Hall before finally reaching the two rows of cabins that flanked either side of the main trail into the woods.

"Which one?" George asked.

"That one," Brian answered, pointing to the one he and Barry had entered earlier. "It's the one furthest away from the woods and there is more moonlight around it."

George nodded, hurried up the steps, and entered the cabin, the rest of them on his heels. Once inside, Brian quietly shut the door and locked it. He then grabbed a nearby dresser and tried to drag it in front of the door. It was solid and heavy, so much so he was having trouble moving it.

"George, help me out here," he said.

George handed the light to Dana and made his way over. It wasn't easy, but the two of them managed to move the dresser, barricading the door.

"What the heck is in this thing?" George asked, pulling open one of the drawers.

Inside was an old heavy quilt.

"Anybody cold?" George asked sarcastically. It was, after all, late July.

"What's in the other drawers?" Brian asked curiously.

George looked and found more blankets. "I don't see where these would be of much use to us right now," he muttered regretfully.

Brian peered around the room. "I don't know about that," he said hopefully. "These windows are open and anyone outside can look in here and see us."

"But if we cover them..." Dana said, her words trailing off.

George nodded and tossed a blanket to her, and then another to Brian. He then took one himself and the three of them went about covering the windows while Andi, Nicole and Barry sat on the floor, huddled together, seemingly paralyzed with fear.

Dana shined the light around the now much darker room and noticed something of interest on a high shelf. "Jack pot," she said, hurrying over to the shelf. She reached up and pulled down a glass lantern with plenty of oil still inside it.

"Great," Brian said. "Now has anyone got a light?"

Dana walked over to Andi and held out her hand. Andi sniffed, retrieved the lighter from her jean shorts pocket, and held it up. Dana took it and the lantern over to the nearby desk where she lit it. Suddenly, a dim orange light filled the room. Somehow, Brian thought this made him feel slightly safer. He looked down at Andi and couldn't help but feel pity for her. She was no longer the brash, bad girl that she was just a short time ago. She was fragile, vulnerable and seemingly on the edge of losing it completely. He knelt down beside her.

"Andi, I know this is probably tough, but we need to know what happened," he said. "We've got to have some idea of what we're up against."

She shivered as if the question had triggered an unsettling memory. Then she slowly turned her head to look at him. "Mossback," she whispered. "He's real."

Brian felt a chill run up his spine. He noticed Barry listening intently to her and wished he wasn't. In that moment he'd given nearly anything for the chance to restart the entire day. If he could've, they'd both be sitting in a movie theater instead of an old campground with a crazed monster hunting them. He forced the thought aside and returned his attention to Andi. "Are you sure?" he replied. "Did you see him?"

She swallowed and shivered again. "Not really," she answered. "It was too dark, but I heard him breathing. I heard him moving and I could even smell him. My god he was so big."

"How did you get away?" Brian asked, hoping he wasn't prodding too far with the questions.

"I-I ran when it grabbed h-him," she stammered. "I could h-hear it killing him."

Tears began streaming down her cheeks again and when she went to wipe them away, she smeared the flecks of blood that she probably had no idea were all over her face. Brian resisted his own urge to tear up as he heard her describe the horrifying things she heard the monster did to Mark and his screaming when it was happening.

"It threw what was left of him like he was nothing more than a rag doll," she said, barely above a whisper. "He landed right in front of me."

"That's enough," Nicole said curtly. "I don't want to hear any more of this."

Brian nodded and agreed. He reached out and put a hand on Andi's shoulder, giving her a gentle squeeze, hoping somehow it would provide her with an inkling of comfort.

"Brian, come here," George suddenly called out from the far corner of the room.

He hurried over to him, worried that he'd seen or heard something. "What's wrong?"

"Nothing," George said, turning slightly away from him, keeping his voice low. "We just need to discuss what we're going to do."

"Honestly, man, I think we just need to sit tight right now," Brian replied quietly.

George's brow furrowed. "No, I don't think so," he said. "We're sitting ducks if we just wait here and do nothing. Whoever–or whatever, is out there isn't just going to go away."

Brian shrugged. "I don't know, up to this point the only people that have gotten hurt have been in the vicinity of that old water tower. I don't think it wants anyone around it. If we just stay away from it–"

"No," George cut in. "Did you forget that it's been right here in the campground? Who do you think did that damage to your car? A squirrel?"

Brian sighed, realizing he was right. And George wasn't even aware of Dana's claims that she saw something moving around in the shadows right before dusk. That had been right near the Dining Hall. The unfortunate reality was that whatever was out there, wasn't just hanging around the water tower, it had only killed there.

"Well, what are you proposing we do?" Brian asked, ready to hear him out.

"I just would feel a lot better hiding out in this cabin if we had a way to defend ourselves," he replied. "Right now, we have nothing but a flashlight, some blankets, and a lantern. There's gotta be something else around her we could use."

Brian thought about it. "I've got a pocketknife. And maybe there's a baseball bat around here. Surely, they played baseball during camp."

George smiled. "Now you're talking," he muttered. If anyone in the group was comfortable with a baseball bat, it was him. "It's too bad I didn't bring my truck because I've got one behind the seat."

"I guess if there is going to be one around here it would be in one of the other cabins," Brian said. "Or maybe there's a storage closet somewhere. The main office is way back near the gate, that's way too far for us to try to get to."

"Maybe there's a closet in the Dining Hall," George suggested.

Brian thought back to his brief visit into the Dining Hall to dry off, and then it hit him.

"A knife!" he said, his voice now loud enough for the others to hear. "And not just any knife, there was a big one in the kitchen. One of those like Michael Myers uses in that movie!"

"Well, that's it, then," George replied. "We've got to get that knife."

"Oh no you're not," Dana interjected as she began to realize what they were plotting. "We all need to stay right here until the sun comes up."

George scratched his head and glared at her. "Until the sun comes up?" he asked, his eyes wide. "Dana, do you think this thing is a vampire? What difference does that make?"

"Well at least we could see better," she explained. "And I always heard the original murders occurred at night."

"That's true," Brian said, recalling his conversation with Uncle Chuck.

George moved a hand to his face and rubbed his eyes. "What are you suggesting?" he asked wearily. "Do you really think the killer from 1958–Mossback, or whoever it was, is back doing it all over again? Twenty-five years have passed!"

"Twenty-five years to the day," Brian said. "Don't you think that's a little eerie?"

"Of course it is," he answered. "But I really think if we just sit here all-night waiting for the sunrise, we're not going to make it. I'm going for that knife."

"This is a bad idea," Dana said, still standing firm on her opinion.

"He can't go alone," Nicole said, rising from the floor. "I know George, and there's no talking him out of this. He's going to go, but I don't think he should go alone."

Brian sighed uneasily. "Fine," he muttered. "I'll go with him."

"No," Andi said, still seated on the floor. She looked panicked. "You and George are the biggest of all of us that are left. One of you should stay behind to make sure we have a chance to fight back."

The boys looked at each other.

"She's right," George said. "Brian, you need to stay with them. You know...just in case."

"I don't want you to leave," Barry said. It sounded like a plea instead of a suggestion.

"Fine, I'm not going anywhere," he replied to his brother. "But I still don't think George should either."

George reached for the dresser. "Help me move it back a little so I can get out." With reluctance, Brian helped him.

"If you're going to do it, please go straight there and straight back," he said when they cracked the door open.

"I'm going too," Nicole said abruptly.

They all looked at her.

"I told you he shouldn't go alone," she said. "If no one else is going, I will."

Dana stepped toward her. "Nicole, I really–"

"Dana, I don't want to hear it," she said, briskly walking over to where George was. "I'm going with him. It's settled."

Brian and Dana exchanged glances. Both of them knew there was no talking either of them out of it.

"Just hurry back," Brian said, sounding defeated.

George squeezed through the opening and then waited for Nicole on the front porch. Once she was outside, he leaned back to the door so only Brian could hear him speak.

"If we're not back in ten minutes, do not come looking for us."

Brian blinked at him as the gravity of his words set in. "Hurry up," he replied, shoving the flashlight into his hand.

Chapter Twelve

"That was so sad," Sara said as she peered into the mirror that was set inside the back of the sun visor. Her makeup needed freshening up and she knew that the drive to the diner would be a short one. She'd have to work fast.

"Yeah, despite the oddness of it all, it's hard reliving it," Chuck replied as he gently wheeled the car toward downtown Darkwood.

"For many years I felt a lot of guilt," Sara said as she carefully applied a light coating of foundation to her face. "I felt guilty for surviving and being able to go on and live my life while the others did not."

"That's not an uncommon thing for people that went through what we experienced," Chuck said. "But we couldn't just stop living. Our friends wouldn't have wanted us to give up."

"I know that," she said. "And I'd pretty much put it behind me. But going to the memorial and seeing all their loved ones…a flood of emotions came back."

"Yeah, I felt it too," he admitted. "And now I've got all this anxiety because I have no idea what Sheriff Turner wants to talk to us about."

Sara put away her blush and reached for her lipstick inside her make up bag. She suddenly paused to look over at him. "You don't think there's been some kind of new development in the case that he wants to tell us about, do you?"

Chuck cocked his head. "I'd be lying if I said it didn't cross my mind," he confessed. "Why else would the new sheriff want to meet with us?"

Sara pondered the question for a moment and could think of no other reasonable answer. She applied her lipstick just as they entered the parking lot.

Chuck parked right beside Sheriff Howard Turner's boxy police cruiser. The car was white with a large gold star emblazoned on the doors. The red and blue light bar that stretched across the roof was oversized, Chuck thought, and would have no problem getting someone's attention when turned on. He exited the vehicle and then waited for Sara to walk around to meet him, at which point he took her hand and led her to the long porch that took up the entire front of the building. There were bright lights illuminating the porch to the point they could only see the sheriff's silhouette.

"Are y'all sure this is an okay place to meet?" he asked as they approached. He had taken his cowboy hat off and was turning it in his hands. Sheriff Turner was at least ten years younger than them and his boyish face made him appear even younger than that.

"It's absolutely fine," Chuck replied.

"Okay, well, I picked it because I didn't figure they'd be real busy tonight," the sheriff explained. "I didn't want us to go to some crowded place where we couldn't even hear ourselves think. That said, if you don't like the food here–"

"Seriously, this is fine," Chuck said, cutting him off.

Turner nodded, and then held the door open, motioning for them to enter. Once inside, a young waitress with bad skin greeted them and gestured for them to follow her.

"What'll you have to drink?" the waitress asked as they all scooted into the booth. Her voice was monotone and suggested she was probably nearing the end of her shift, ready to go home. Turner and Chuck ordered sweet tea while Sara requested water with a lemon. The waitress slapped three menus onto the table and then mumbled something incoherent as she walked away.

"She's a real ray of sunshine," Chuck said as the waitress strolled away.

"I'll say," Sara agreed with a chuckle.

"Yeah, she's my sister," Sheriff Turner grunted as he grabbed a menu.

Chuck and Sara looked at each other; both of them feeling their faces get hot from embarrassment.

"I'm sorry," Chuck said. "I didn't know—"

Turner held up a hand and smiled. "Stop," he said smiling. "I said she's my sister, I never said I disagreed with your assessment of her. You're right, she's rude as hell."

"Well, still," Sara replied. "Chuck shouldn't have said that."

"Really, it's fine," he said, waving her off. "She'll be back in a minute to get our order. That's what she mumbled when she walked away. Frankly, I don't think she's usually that bad, but since it's me—well, she's never liked it when I come in here. She thinks I'm here to spy on her…long story. Anyway, enough about her, I appreciate you both taking the time to meet with me."

"It's no problem," Chuck said. "We're intrigued to say the least."

Turner nodded and placed his hat on the seat beside him. "I imagine you are, and I don't want to hold you in suspense, so I'll just get right to it."

"Please," Sara said, urging him onward.

He eyed them both for a second and then asked, "Does the name Kevin Parker sound familiar to you?"

Sara felt her heart skip a beat. She glanced over at Chuck and figured he probably had a similar reaction.

"Of course it is," Chuck said. "He's one of the guys that killed Joe Folsom back in 1955."

Sheriff Turner winced at the statement. "Now Chuck," he replied. "That was never proven, and the poor guy lost his mind after that and has been in a mental institution for almost thirty years."

"That's right, Sheriff," Sara said. "And why do you think he snapped? Could it be because the weight of murdering someone and trying to cover it up became too much for him to mentally handle?"

The sheriff took a deep breath and ran a hand over his face. "I deal with facts, not speculation," he replied. "The previous sheriff cleared him of any wrongdoing. It was just an accident."

Chuck laughed. "You mean his father cleared him of wrongdoing. Don't you think the fact that his father was the sheriff is sort of an important part of this story?"

"An investigation was performed by the state," Turner replied. "Ultimately, there was no proof that he actually did anything malicious to that young man. Of course, they had a little scuffle, which happens with boys all time, but murder is a giant leap from that. That said, I believe Kevin felt a lot of guilt about what happened, and he was never the same again. I don't know that he's ever said more than five words in all the time he's spent at the asylum."

Chuck and Sara looked at each other. The truth, that the sheriff didn't seem to be privy to, was that Sara had witnessed the 'scuffle' between Kevin and Joe. She'd seen Joe hit his head on a rock, which had been a direct result of a gut punch that Kevin had given him. What happened to Joe's dying body after it had been left with Kevin and his friend Jamie had always been a mystery, but Sara and Chuck had a pretty good idea. They considered filling Sheriff Turner in on the details he was clearly missing but decided to wait and see where this was going first.

"Sheriff, what's all this about?" Chuck asked. "Why are you bringing up Kevin Parker?"

Before he could answer, the waitress returned to take their orders.

"You know what I want, Becky," Turner said, sliding the menu back over to her.

"I think we just want a couple of burgers and fries," Sara said.

"So, you're all just getting the same thing?" she asked, blinking.

"Sounds like it, thanks sis," Turner said dismissively.

She rolled her eyes, scooped up the menus, and then trudged away. Once out of earshot, the sheriff continued.

"Kevin Parker has been obsessed with everything concerning the murders of the counselors in 1958. He's also been obsessed with the legend of Mossback," he said. "It's almost like it's the only thing that keeps him going. For twenty-five years he's filled notebooks with drawings and notes about the murders, Mossback, and...," he paused and shifted uneasily in his seat.

"And what?" Chuck asked.

"Well, he seems to mention Sara a lot too," he said, peering over at her.

"What? Why me?" she asked, pointing at herself.

The sheriff shrugged. "I mean, you're the only survivor," he replied.

"That's not true," she shot back, grabbing Chuck's arm. "He was a survivor too."

Sheriff Turner looked out the window and sighed. "You're right," he said. "That hadn't really occurred to me."

Chuck glanced over at Sara. It didn't take him long at all to put it together. Sara was the only survivor that had witnessed Kevin's assault of Joe Folsom, he thought. That was the difference. Surely Sara knew that too.

"Maybe there's something else to it, then," the sheriff continued, thinking aloud.

They just stared at him as he continued to think, waiting to learn more as it certainly seemed like there was more, he wanted to share. Finally, the sheriff scratched at the back of his neck and shook his head. "I suppose ultimately that part doesn't matter. I told you all that because as of this morning there has been a new development that I wanted to make sure you both were aware of. Before I tell you this, please know that we're on top of it and there is nothing to be worried about."

They both leaned forward, and Chuck felt Sara's grip on his arm tighten.

"Well, by all means, please tell us," She said anxiously.

Chapter Thirteen

George and Nicole moved quickly and methodically across the open space in the campground.

"Stay in the shadow as much as you can," George whispered as he glanced up at the bright moon looming overhead.

"I'm right behind you," Nicole said. "Just hurry."

George paused and looked back at her. "It's not too late for you to go back to the cabin," he said. "You don't have to go with me."

"I'm fine, just go," she said, her eyes pleading.

George grunted but did as he was told. When they reached the double door entrance to the dining hall, he crouched down and reached for the handle. Nicole suddenly reached out and grabbed his arm.

"Wait," she said.

He looked at her, bewildered.

"How do we know Mossback isn't in there?"

George's mouth dropped open, and he rolled his eyes. "Nicole, go back to the cabin," he muttered, pointing. "I know you're scared."

She shook her head and put on a brave face. "No way, I'm staying. I'm just thinking we should have a plan if he's in there."

"The truth is, if he is in there, we're probably screwed," he replied. "That reason alone is why you should go back."

"Shut up," she snapped. "I'm not going back. But I'm serious, what do we do if he's in there?"

"If he's in there, as soon as we see him, we run like hell," he said. "That's the plan. Got it?"

She huffed and looked away. "Great plan."

George again reached for the door and gently pulled it open. The dented doors looked as if they'd been forced open, and recently. Not a good sign, he thought as his mind began to race. He swiftly moved inside and held the door open for Nicole. She came in and duck-walked around him so he could ease the door shut behind her to keep it from making a sound. When they were both inside and the door was shut, he flicked on the flashlight and shone the beam around the room. For the most part, the vast room was empty except for a couple of fold up tables that were leaning against a wall to the left. On the right side there were chairs stacked on top of each other. Straight ahead of them, in the center of the back wall, were two more doors that he guessed led to the kitchen.

"I don't think anyone is in here," Nicole said, sounding relieved.

George listened for any sounds that would indicate movement or a presence of any kind. Despite his best efforts to pick up any sound at all, he heard nothing. It was an encouraging sign but the adrenaline he felt pumping through his body wouldn't allow him to relax, even for a moment.

"Let's get this over with," he muttered, standing.

George walked briskly to the door and opened it. He held the light out in front of him and allowed the beam to wash over the room in every direction that he pointed it.

"Do you see the knife?" he asked, squinting.

Nicole reluctantly moved past him for a better look. The kitchen was surprisingly barren, but the counters, stove, and refrigerator remained. On the wall beside the stove, she caught a glimpse of something dark hanging on the wall.

"There," she said, pointing.

George spotted the knife and made a beeline for it, snatching it off the wall. "Brian wasn't kidding," he said, looking it over. "This thing looks like it's straight out of *Halloween*."

Suddenly a sound was heard from the dining area that made them both freeze instantly.

"What the heck was that?" Nicole said, afraid to even blink.

"Sounded like a tin can on the floor," George replied. "Maybe it was a rat or something. I'm sure this place has had all kinds of wildlife in it over the past two and a half decades."

She slowly looked over at him. "We need to see if there is a back door. I'm not going in there," she said, jerking a thumb toward the swinging doors that led into the dining area.

George nodded and moved the light to the back wall again, slower this time, in search of a door. They both noticed the glint of a doorknob at the same moment and rushed toward it like mosquitoes noticing a neon sign. George opened it and found a short hallway that led to yet another door. He felt confident that it was the exit they were looking for.

Nicole squeaked suddenly, sounding startled.

"What is it?" he asked, frantically looking back at her.

"I heard something," she said. "I think someone is definitely out there."

"Close the door," George said, but he didn't wait for her to do it. He reached out, pulled it shut, and then twisted the lock on the knob. They were now contained in the short hallway between doors.

Then they heard another sound, this one much more terrifying.

"Someone just came through the swinging doors," Nicole whispered.

George didn't hesitate. He immediately reached for the next door, twisted the knob, and pulled.

"Oh no," he muttered in disbelief.

"What do you mean 'oh no'," she snapped. "What's wrong?"

"The deadbolt is locked," he said. He again twisted the knob and pulled, praying he was wrong.

"So, unlock it!"

"I can't, there's only a keyhole on this side," he replied.

Suddenly the knob on the other door began to jiggle. Someone was trying to turn it.

Nicole's eyes widened. "Oh my god," she said as her heart rate picked up. She barged past him, trying the door herself. When it wouldn't open, she began pounding on it.

"What are you doing, stop!" George said. "He'll hear us!"

The knob began to jiggle more violently.

"It's too late!" Nicole wailed. "We've got to get out of here!"

She stepped back and kicked the door. It didn't budge.

"Take the light and move out of the way!" George said as he handed off the flashlight and shoved the knife into his back pocket. He then threw his shoulder into the door with all the force he could muster. It moved only slightly.

"Do it again," Nicole urged. Suddenly there was a loud crash behind her. She could see the wood beginning to splinter in the center of the other door. "Hurry up!"

George moved back as far as he could and then ran forward, lunging his entire body into the door. Again, he noticed progress. Before he could try once more, Nicole screamed. He looked back and could see a large arm now reaching in through a ragged hole in the other door. The arm was massive and covered in dirt and grime. It reached out, blindly grasping for anyone it could grab.

"George, hurry!"

He began kicking the door as hard as he could in the spot where the doorknob and deadbolt met the jamb. In the dancing beam of light, he could see the wood beginning to break apart. Thankfully, it finally gave way as Nicole's shrill screaming made his ears ring. The broken door swung open, and he ran through it into the cool night air. Once outside, he yanked the knife from his back pocket and looked back, expecting to see Nicole right behind him, but to his horror she was gone. The other door had been opened, and she'd undoubtedly been pulled back into the kitchen. He stood there for a long moment, the knife twitching in his shaking hand as he contemplated what to do.

"Nicole!"

No answer.

George gripped the knife tightly, willing himself to calm down. He took a deep breath and slowly walked back toward the open door. As he moved, he listened carefully for any sound that would alert him to danger. Once in the hallway he again called out to her but again received no answer. He reached down to pick up the flashlight that lay on the floor, still shining brightly. When he reached the second door, George slowly poked his head out to peer into the kitchen. He didn't see anything or anyone in the darkness so, with great reluctance, he shone the beam of light into the blackness for a better look. To his great relief he saw no sign of a threat, but he did notice the mangled body of Nicole lying on the tiled floor, blood pooling around her head. Her pink sweatshirt was also spattered with blood. There was so much of it that George was unable to tell where on her body she'd actually suffered an injury. He started to approach her lifeless body but knew it was pointless, and under the circumstances, reckless. There was nothing he could do for her now, but what he could do was save himself.

With tears in his eyes, George turned away and ran back through the hallway toward the exterior yet again. He began to play out in his head how he'd tell the others about Nicole. He wondered if they'd blame him for her death. He was already blaming himself, after all. As soon as George stepped back into the night, a hulking figure stepped in front of him, startling him so badly he dropped the flashlight; it fell, clanging to the sidewalk under his feet. The being appeared to be dark in color and stunk like a wild animal. Shadow covered its face which made it all the more ominous–a faceless harbinger of death.

George knew he only had one way out of the dire predicament, and despite the overwhelming feeling of terror that washed over him, he raised the large knife and charged at the being he knew would kill him if he fled. The figure raised an arm, and George was surprised at how quickly it moved. The arm met the knife as it plunged downward, piercing flesh and coming to a sickening stop. George had somehow managed to impale his attacker's forearm with the knife. He heard a grunt, but he wasn't sure if it originated out of pain or anger. George then tried to pull the knife out so that he could inflict more damage, but to his shock, it didn't move. The next thing he knew, a large grimy hand was thrust forward, and he felt thick fingers wrap quickly around his neck. The squeeze that followed was so powerful, George would've sworn it was machinery had he not known better. He felt his windpipe collapse as the pressure increased and then the fingers began to tear through the skin, cartilage and flesh. The stinging sensation and the ripping sound that followed, as his neck became obliterated to the point that his head began to separate from the rest of his body, was mercifully short. George's eyes drifted upward, and he watched the stars disappear from the night sky for the final time. The world around him faded away.

Chapter Fourteen

"Sheriff, please hurry," Sara said, urging him to speed up.

He glanced back at her in his mirror. "Ms. Lancaster, it's going to be fine, I assure you. I think you're both overreacting just a little bit."

Chuck winced when he heard the words. He knew how Sara reacted when he'd told her she was 'overreacting' in the past and it never went over well. He knew if he didn't cut into the conversation, things were going to escalate.

"Sheriff, respectfully, I think our concern is more validated than you realize," he said calmly. "We've been trusted with the care of our nephews and this news you've given us, well, we'll feel a hell of a lot better when we put our eyes on those boys again."

Sheriff Turner motored the police cruiser down a tight alleyway in an effort to save some time, though he genuinely did not believe the boys were in any real danger.

"So, what are you going to do when we arrive?" he asked. "You're going to pull those poor kids out of their movie before it's finished?"

"Yes," Sara said quickly. She crossed her arms and looked out the window. The passing streetlights strobed over her face. "No," she said, thinking. "I don't know, maybe. I just want to make sure they're okay right now."

"I'm telling you, they're fine," he said, smirking.

"I'm glad that you find this amusing," Sara said.

The sheriff's mouth immediately straightened. "I'm sorry, I–"

"Because if anything happens to those boys, I'm going to hold you responsible," she snapped, cutting him off.

Chuck turned in the front seat to look back at her. "Sara, everything is going to be fine," he said, trying to ease her obvious anxiety. "We'll get them back home and we won't let them out of our sight until this is all over."

Sara huffed and kept her arms crossed. She held herself tightly. "I just don't understand why you waited so long to tell us," She said, her gaze set on the back of Sheriff Turner's head.

He shrugged. "Because I didn't see any imminent danger," he admitted.

She shook her head and looked away, resisting the urge to scream at him.

They finally reached the movie theater, and the sheriff parked the car directly in front of the sidewalk that led to the front entrance. They all clambered out and briskly made their way to the ticket booth. A young man with jet black hair and horn-rimmed glasses stared at them uneasily through the glass.

"Can I help you?" he asked a bit meekly.

Sheriff Turner flashed a friendly smile to hopefully make the kid relax. "Yes, you can," he said. "We're looking for a couple of kids that came here tonight to see…," he paused, thinking.

"*Jaws 3-D*," Chuck said from behind him.

Turner snapped his fingers. "Right," he said. "One of them was seventeen, the other thirteen. They're two brothers so they resemble one another. Both of them have hair about the same color as yours. The younger kid was wearing an Inspector Gadget t-shirt."

The kid glanced at his wristwatch. "It looks like *Jaws* is about to end," he muttered. "I saw a lot of boys come in here tonight that meet that description. They should all come filing out of there real soon."

Sheriff Turner looked back at Chuck. "What do you want to do?" he asked. "I mean I'd hate to go in there and interrupt the ending for everyone in there."

Chuck sighed and glanced over at Sara. He knew what she wanted to do.

"Honey," he said. "I don't think it'll hurt to wait a few more minutes."

She frowned and her eyes narrowed. "Fine, you two wait here. I'm going to look for Brian's car in the parking lot."

She turned and strode away from them, her heels clicking on the sidewalk. Sheriff Turner reached over and grabbed Chuck's shoulder.

"Don't worry," he said. "She's gonna feel better in just a few minutes."

Chuck smiled a bit nervously. "Yeah, I hope so," he said.

Sara walked briskly along the sidewalk that ran down and around the building to the parking lot in the back. Once there, she scanned over the assorted variety of vehicles, searching frantically for the orange Pinto. When she didn't see it, she began running down the aisles for a better look. It was, after all, a very small car. The search took several minutes but when she'd weaved her way through the entire lot, she stopped and rested next to a light pole at the edge of the lot, her breathing labored from all the running. To her dismay, she saw no sign of any orange cars, much less a Ford Pinto. As her mind began to play out the worst possibilities she could imagine in her head, she heard Chuck call out to her.

"Do you see the car?"

She peered at him and noticed Sheriff Turner standing alongside him, looking slightly less calm than he'd been. She did all she could to hide her growing concern and shook her head in response. They jogged over to her, and she could tell by their body language that the boys had not been in the movie theater.

"Something's wrong," she said, swallowing back her fear. "I can feel it."

"Don't worry, we're going to find them," Sheriff Turner said. "I've put out an APB so every officer I've got is on the lookout. I'm personally going to go and check the Camp Beaver Brook campground to make sure they're not there."

Sara snapped her attention to Chuck. "Surely Brian wouldn't have–"

Chuck reached out, grabbing her by the shoulders. "I did my best to scare him into staying as far away from there as possible, so I doubt they're there, but given the fact that I heard about a teenage party going on there tonight, it's worth a look," he said.

"Well then we need to go with you," Sara said, pulling away from Chuck so she could look Turner in the eyes.

The sheriff shifted on his feet uncomfortably. "I can't let you do that," he said flatly.

Her eyes narrowed and she stepped closer to him. "Excuse me?"

"Ms. Lancaster, it's not safe for civilians to go on patrol with me," he said, moving his eyes away from her. "My deputy is on the way here now to pick y'all up and take you back to your vehicle. He will then follow you home. I also instructed him to sit with you there while we figure this out."

"Sit with us, or hold us captive?" she asked, her anger clearly growing.

"To protect you," Turner shot back.

"Maybe we could be of some help," Chuck said. "You'll need help to search the campground."

"If they've been out there tonight, there will be signs," he replied. "If I feel that I need help, I assure you I'll call for it. This isn't negotiable. I feel some responsibility for the both of you right now and I don't want to put either of you in a risky spot."

"I thought you were assuring us that there is nothing to worry about," Sara clapped back. "You've said that numerous times."

"She's right," Chuck said, raising an eyebrow.

Sheriff Turner kicked a rock in front of him and shook his head. "I still stand by everything I've said," he muttered. "But under the circumstances, it doesn't hurt to err on the side of caution. Besides, you may get home and find that the boys are already there."

Just then another police cruiser rolled up to the curb, brakes squeaking.

"That's your ride," Turner said, motioning toward the car.

Chuck sighed, hooked an arm under Sara's and led her toward the car. "We'll talk about what we're going to do when we get to our car," he said in a voice just above a whisper.

He didn't want to go home, and he knew she didn't either. But it was obvious that the sheriff wasn't going to back down from his stance. They'd be better off getting away from him so they could figure out how they were going to proceed. What both of them knew, but wouldn't dare say, was that they had no intention of standing idly by while Brian and Barry were missing.

Chapter Fifteen

"What is taking them so long?" Dana asked worriedly. She peeked out of the window but was careful to only move the curtain enough so that she could see. Outside, the open spaces between the buildings and playground were empty. The shadows from the trees that projected onto the ground from the moon overhead stretched toward their cabin like ghostly fingers, reaching for them and getting ever so closer with each passing minute.

"I think something's off. I've got a bad feeling about this," Brian admitted, though he hoped he was wrong.

"Brian, I want to go home," Barry said, standing.

He'd been seated next to Andi in the middle of the floor. She'd been eerily and unusually quiet. Barry had been mostly silent too and Brian could tell his brother was terrified.

"I know, Barry," he replied. "I'm working on it." He walked over to the window where Dana was. "Still no sign of them at all?" he asked.

She shook her head and gave him a look of dread. "It's been well over ten minutes. Something happened to them," she whispered.

Brian closed his eyes and sighed, feeling the weight of what he had to do press down on him. "I'm going to go check it out," he said.

"Brian, no," Dana said forcefully. "George even told you not to go looking for them."

"And when have I ever let George boss me around? We know where they went so, I'm going straight there just to have a look, and I'll come straight back."

"That's an extraordinarily bad idea," she said. "I can't let you do it."

He smiled at her. "Well, you can't stop me, Dana."

Brian reached for the door, and she grabbed his arm. "Don't," she said. "Please."

He could see the fear in her eyes and though he knew she had concerns about him, he was also cognizant of the fact that if he left, she was now the one Andi and Barry would look to for guidance. That seemed to be weighing on her just as much as her own fear.

"I'll be back," he said. "I promise. Just look after Barry for me."

Dana said nothing but her expression was pleading with him not to leave. He ignored it and opened the door to step out. Barry noticed and ran over to him.

"Where are you going?"

Brian knelt slightly. "I'll be right back," he said, and then he leaned in close. "Watch after these girls, I'm counting on you."

Barry took a deep breath and nodded slowly. He had no choice but to put on a brave face now that Brian had bestowed such an important responsibility upon him. Brian winked at him and eased outside, closing the door behind him. Once outside, he crept along the darkest areas within the edge of the woods and made his way to the front of the dining hall. The entrance was unfortunately bathed in full moonlight and would put him in a very vulnerable position if he stepped toward it. Brian looked around in all directions, straining his eyes for any sign of movement. When he finally felt comfortable enough to leave the relative safety of the shadowed woods, he ran to the entrance and quickly pulled the door open to step inside. Once he was in the building, he stood in the foyer for a long time looking around the vast dining area for any sign of George, Nicole, or worse.

He resisted the urge to call out to them and instead padded quietly across the tiled floor to the double doors that led into the kitchen. Brian immediately regretted not bringing the other flashlight. It was significantly darker in the kitchen and for a moment he couldn't see anything, but then he noticed a very faint light coming from the back. He soon realized there was another open door and a hallway beyond it.

Carefully, he strode toward the hallway, taking great care with each step to avoid tripping or ramming his shin into something painful. When he finally reached the doorway, he noticed another door at the end of the hall that led to the exterior. The flashlight that George had taken lay on the ground, its bulb shining brightly across the dew-covered grass. A terrible, sickening feeling began to swell deep in his gut, and he broke out into a cold sweat. Despite every fiber of his being screaming at him to flee, Brian stepped forward so he could get a better view outside of the door. When he stepped out, he immediately noticed the lifeless body of George Valentine lying on the ground about twenty yards away.

Brian slowly knelt and picked up the flashlight, keeping his head on a swivel as he did. Mossback had to be close and if he didn't want to be the next victim he needed to get away as soon as he could. With the flashlight gripped tightly in his hand, Brian pointed the light toward George, and it was then he realized his head was no longer attached to his body. All that remained was a ragged, bloody stem of a neck protruding from the blue tank top he was wearing.

Brian felt his knees get weak and before he knew it, he'd collapsed to the ground. The terrible feeling in his gut was now in overdrive and he began to vomit. The fear that gripped him made him shake violently but he willed himself back to his feet. He caught a glimpse of something shiny on the ground and quickly realized it was the knife that George had come for. There was blood on it, but there was no way to be certain whose it was. Brian suddenly felt an eerie sensation that unsettled him. It was the feeling of being watched. Quickly, he scooped up the knife and turned to head back to the cabin. No sooner had he turned his back, than the sound of someone approaching in the woods behind him began.

With reluctance, Brian glanced over his shoulder and did so just in time to see a dark figure moving toward him and obviously picking up speed. His heart skipped a beat and the weakness in his knees returned. Brian steadied himself on the side of the building but knew there was no time to gather himself back up. Instead, he began to run, and the figure gave chase.

As Brian rounded the corner of the building, a thought occurred to him. If he continued on to the cabin, he'd lead his pursuer right to Dana, Barry and Andi. It would be best, he decided, to seek refuge elsewhere. With limited options, he headed down the hill and toward the lake. He moved so fast; his legs could barely keep up and he nearly fell at least twice. He looked back again to see where the pursuing figure was and found that the dreadful being was still marching toward him.

Brian glanced at the pier that led out into the lake and almost ran on it, but he caught himself. That would be stupid, he thought. Where could he go once, he reached the end of the pier? He instead turned, taking the trail that winded along the shoreline to the west. The flashlight showed the way, but Brian knew if there was any chance of losing his attacker, eventually he'd have to turn it off. Soon, he knew he'd have to venture into the woods. But then another thought occurred to him. What if that's exactly what his attacker would want him to do? The forest, after all, had seemingly been the domain of Mossback for over two decades now. Was it really the best place for him to go? The light danced ahead of him as he ran and suddenly, he caught a glimpse of something that seemingly answered his question. It was a small boat, turned upside down in a manner that suggested the last person that had used it didn't want to leave it where it would fill up with rainwater. Brian stopped and quickly turned the boat over. This uncovered a black snake that quickly slithered away, making its escape right between his legs. Brian yelped in startled surprise but didn't stop. With the boat overturned and now halfway in the water, he jumped into it. He looked over and gasped as the dark figure loomed over him, mere feet away now. Brian raised his leg and pushed his foot against a nearby tree at the edge of the water, propelling him away from the shore. The figure lunged for the boat, swinging a large arm outward in an attempt to grab it but his fingers just missed it. The little boat glided across the surface of the lake into deeper water and Brian breathed a sigh of relief.

The dark figure stood on the shoreline and just stared at Brian. The dim light made it impossible to see his expression, but Brian knew the being was scowling angrily at him. He could literally feel the rage filled eyes burning into him. Then, suddenly, the figure stepped forward into the water and began wading toward him. It was then that the boat coasted to almost a complete stop and Brian realized there were no oars on board. Frantic, he leaned over, nearly toppling the boat over. He plunged a hand into the cold water and began paddling, desperate to put as much distance between him and his attacker as possible. Unfortunately, the boat moved very little, and the being trudged ever so closer. The water was up to the figure's chest and Brian began to seriously consider jumping into the water to swim away. It was then something quite unexpected happened. Bright strobing lights of blue and red began to swirl around them. A police cruiser casually rolled into the gravel parking lot next to the campground, coming to a stop just behind Brian's car.

Chapter Sixteen

"Oh my god, I don't believe it," Dana said, suddenly feeling a tremendous wave of relief wash over her.

"What is it?" Andi asked, rising to her feet for the first time in quite a while. "What do you see?"

Dana looked back at her from the window. "It's a police car!"

Andi smiled and reached over to hug Barry. "Thank god," she muttered. "This nightmare can finally end."

"But where's Brian?" Barry asked, obviously concerned.

"I'm sure he's fine," Dana answered, forcing a smile and praying it was true.

Sheriff Howard Turner opened the car door, and it squeaked in protest. He winced at the noise. It aggravated him. The car had been damaged six months earlier in a minor fender bender that occurred during a short high-speed chase he'd been involved in. The body shop repaired the car–or so he thought. It looked well enough, but the god-awful squeaking that occurred every time he opened the door drove him crazy as it was obvious something wasn't lining up right on the body. Now that he stood in the crisp night air of what was left of Camp Beaver Brook, he began to feel like something wasn't right there either.

"Hello?" he called out. "Brian Lancaster, are you here?"

The sheriff pulled a flashlight from the car, switched it on, and then shone a beam of light around his surroundings. The sound of a door opening from somewhere close by alarmed him and he reached for his revolver.

"Hello! Sheriff!"

It was a female's voice; not at all what he was expecting.

"Come out here and show yourself," Turner said, now holding the gun in one hand and the flashlight in the other.

A young brunette wearing a yellow blouse and white shorts stepped out. She was holding her hands up, obviously trying to show that she was harmless, and her face wore an expression of fear and relief. Two more figures followed her out of the shadows. Another young girl, this one blonde, and next to her was a young boy wearing an Inspector Gadget t-shirt.

"Are you all okay?" Turner asked, lowering his weapon.

The question seemed to trigger the brunette, and she began to cry. "No," she muttered. "We're not! Our friends have been killed."

"Killed?" he asked, his voice rising as his worst fears began to materialize. He began looking around in all directions, his eyes scanning everything. "Who killed them?" he asked.

"It was Mossback," the young boy called out. "Mossback is out here!"

The sheriff stared at him, unsure how to respond. In his mind, Mossback wasn't real but now was not the time to argue with children. "Son, is your name Barry?"

The boy nodded.

"Get over here, all of you," he said, motioning with the gun for them to come to him. "Are any of you hurt?"

"No, but Barry's older brother Brian is missing," Dana said. "He left us just a little while ago to look for George and Nicole. He should have been back by now."

"Okay, I want the three of you to wait in the car," the sheriff said. His eyes were still darting around. "I'll find Brian and your friends."

Dana and Barry quickly made their way into the backseat while Andi took the front. Before she closed the door, the sheriff said, "Keep the doors locked until I get back. Do you understand?"

Dana looked at him, tears still streaming down her face. "Don't you think you should call for more help?" she asked.

Turner smiled at her. "Honey, everything is going to be fine. Close the door and lock it."

Dana stared at him for a moment more. It was as if she believed she was looking at him for the final time and it sent a shiver up his spine. When she finally did close the door, he watched her lock it and offered one more reassuring smile. Dana didn't smile back.

Sheriff Turner turned away and began walking toward the large structure directly ahead of him. The beam from his flashlight shone on the sign that dangled from the side of the building.

"Dining Hall," he said aloud, remembering that this was the building where the bodies of the deceased camp counselors were discovered all those years ago.

Suddenly, he heard someone call out to him from further away. It was a young man's voice, but he was unable to make out what was said.

"Brian Lancaster, is that you?" Turner yelled.

The voice was still hard to hear but he made out one unmistakable word: *Help*.

Turner rushed down the hill toward the voice. He shined his light ahead of him and could see the dark waters of Beaver Brook Lake. Directly in front of him was an old pier that, based on a quick glance, he doubted was safe to walk out on. Despite his reservations, he carefully made his way across the rickety planks that took him further out over the water. If he didn't know better, it sounded like the voice he heard came from somewhere in the middle of the lake. When he reached the end of the pier he glanced right, then left, following the illumination that poured out of his flashlight. There was a thick mist that rolled over the still water. It made it even harder to see anyone.

"Over here," the voice said.

"Are you Brian Lancaster?" Turner replied, moving the light.

"Yes," he answered anxiously. "I'm out here in a boat; I don't have any paddles. Watch your back, someone is out there!"

Sheriff Turner looked over his shoulder. Fortunately, there was no one behind him. "Who is out here?" he asked. "Are they trying to hurt you?"

"I don't know who or what it is. It was after me, but took off when you arrived," Brian answered. "It's already killed a couple of my friends for sure. Probably two more that are unaccounted for."

The sheriff took note of Brian's use of the word "it" and it unsettled him. "Okay, well if you're not in any immediate danger, I need to look around. If someone dangerous is out here I need to find them before someone else gets hurt."

Suddenly, Turner heard the sound of a splash under the pier. He immediately pointed his light downward and could see water rippling through the cracks between the boards. He told himself it was nothing more than a fish jumping and turned to head back to shore. No sooner had he taken one step when he heard another splash directly under him. The sheriff pointed the light down again. He still saw rippling water, but also–a shadow?

"Sheriff, you need to run," Brian said, his voice a bit panicked.

"I think it's just fish," Turner replied, still shining his light downward.

What had once been a small shadow in the water suddenly swelled into something large.

"What the hell?" Turner said, leaning down for a better look.

"Sheriff, I really think–"

Brian's sentence was cut off by the sound of splintering wood as a hulking being burst through the pier, directly in the path of Sheriff Turner.

Turner shrieked and stumbled backward onto the pier. The gun fell from his grasp and clattered over the side, falling into the lake. The dark silhouette towered over him, its shoulders rising and falling with each heavy breath. Turner turned away and began to frantically crawl to the end of the pier. Just as he reached it, he felt cold, wet fingers wrapped around his ankle and jerk him violently back. He desperately grasped for anything to hold onto and managed to get his fingers around a plank, momentarily stopping himself from being pulled further. Surprisingly, the grip around his ankle released. Turner rolled onto his back and got a firm grip on his flashlight. It was seemingly the only weapon he had within reach. He'd beat his attacker into submission if that was his only recourse. The being suddenly lunged at him and Turner swung the flashlight, landing a crushing blow to his head. There was a grunt and a recoil. For a brief moment, Turner believed he'd hurt him. Then, to his shock, the being lunged at him again, this time grabbing him around the neck.

Turner began flailing and swinging the flashlight with all his might. The grip around his neck tightened and he felt himself being lifted slightly. Suddenly he was flung downward again and felt his body plunge through the broken pier and into the icy water. The hand around his throat continued to tighten as he was held underwater. Sheriff Turner tried to pull himself free, but it seemed the more he struggled, the tighter the grip became. He could feel himself nearing the point of blacking out, but mercifully, he felt the grip loosen slightly. It was enough for him to take a much-needed breath, and he gasped for the air he desperately craved. Unfortunately, there was no air to be found, only water. His lungs filled quickly, and the painful bite of death came soon after.

"Let him go!" Brian pleaded from the boat as he watched the surreal scene play out before him.

He could not believe how utterly powerful the being was. It had taken the sheriff and slammed his body through the rickety pier as if it were nothing more than paper. Brian could only look on helplessly as the dark entity held the sheriff under the water until he drowned. His pleas were obviously falling on deaf ears.

When it became obvious that Sheriff Turner was dead, the dark silhouette rose and peered coldly at Brian where he sat in the boat, seemingly suggesting he was next. Being on the water was only a temporary safety. He was, after all, completely out in the open. There was no hiding in the middle of the lake. Brian began to paddle with his hands to the nearest shore as the realization that he was on borrowed time began to fully set in. The creature on the pier watched him and Brian feared it would jump into the water and come after him at any moment, but then the blue and red strobing lights from the police car at the camp site got its attention. The dark figure turned away from Brian and began lumbering back toward the camp.

Brian suddenly thought of Barry, Dana and Andi. They'd no doubt seen the sheriff when he arrived. Where were they now? Did they suddenly believe they were safe? The reality was they were anything but.

Chapter Seventeen

"Can you see him?" Barry asked Andi from the back seat.

Andi had the better view from the front, and she craned her head closer to the windshield for a better look. "I can't see anything," she replied. "It's too foggy."

"Relax, Barry," Dana said, sensing his fear. "Everything is fine. The sheriff is trained for stuff like this. He'll be back in a minute and I'm sure he'll have Brian with him."

Barry leaned forward and grasped the metal mesh that separated the front seats from the back. "He's just been gone a really long time," he said, now pressing his face against the mesh. "You still don't see anything?"

Andi squinted, trying to see through the dense fog. "No, I told you it's just too–" She suddenly paused. "Wait a minute, I do see someone coming."

"It's about time," Dana said, beginning to feel relieved. "Do you see Brian?"

"I can't tell yet," she answered. "But it looks like it's just one person. They're definitely coming our way."

"Only one person?" Barry asked worriedly.

"Oh no," Andi said, her tone changing. "Are your doors locked? Lock your doors!"

"What is it?" Dana asked, now her face was pressed on the mesh. "Who do you see?"

"It's not the sheriff and it's not Brian," Andi replied, and she suddenly crouched down to hide.

Dana and Barry instinctively did the same. The approaching silhouette was now upon them, and it loomed large near the passenger side windows.

"It's Mossback," Barry said, a tremor in his voice.

"Shhh," Andi said from the front.

They began to hear the sound of the door handle being pulled from the outside; first from the front door and then the back.

"They're trying to get in," Dana whispered. "Are you sure it's not the sheriff or Brian?"

Andi didn't respond and stayed crouched as low as possible.

Dana slowly raised her head for a better look. The figure outside of the car was large and dark. She couldn't make out any features, but she could see enough to tell it was most definitely not Brian or the sheriff. The large head suddenly turned to look at her and she immediately dropped back down.

There was a long moment of silence and then...pounding. It was on the doors and on the roof of the car. The pounding was loud enough and forceful enough to shake the entire vehicle. Dana resisted the urge to scream, and Barry seemed to sense the importance of keeping quiet as well. Andi, on the other hand, lost complete control. She screamed so loudly that Dana feared the windows would shatter. The pounding grew even louder. The red and blue lights on the roof of the car were destroyed and all at once the strobing ceased. Dana looked on as the shadowy figure then moved around the front of the car to the driver's side. There was more pounding on the door and roof. The sound of the handles being jerked began again. Despite the relentless beating the car had taken, somehow the locks held. Then, just as quickly as it all began, it stopped. There was a long moment of silence before anyone spoke.

"Did he leave?" Dana asked, peering out both sides of the car.

"Why can't we just drive away from here?" Barry asked.

"I already looked for the keys! Don't you think I looked for keys?" Andi said, her voice frantic.

"Calm down, Andi," Dana said, as gently as she could. "He's just scared. We're all scared."

"I just want to get out of here," Barry said. "I just want to go home!"

"We're going to get out of here," Dana said, wrapping her arms around Barry. "I promise."

"You can't promise that," Andi said, glaring at her through the metal mesh. There were tears streaming down her face. "Don't give him false hope."

Dana stared at her. "What are you doing?" she asked, her tone no longer gentle. "You're just giving up now?"

Andi continued to cry; she opened her mouth to speak but stopped. Dana's eyes narrowed and she soon realized that Andi was looking past her, as if something were outside the car behind her. Dana slowly turned around and saw the shadowy figure approaching the car from behind. When it reached the trunk, it stopped and raised something red into the air. It appeared to be a container of some kind. A liquid began to slosh out of the container and suddenly the realization of what was happening dawned on Dana.

"What's that smell?" Barry asked.

"Oh my god," Andi said. "Is that gasoline?"

The figure began walking around the car, still pouring gas on the exterior.

"We've got to get out of here," Dana said, her survival instincts now kicking in.

As the dark figure continued to make its way to the driver side of the vehicle, Dana quickly pulled the handle on the passenger side rear door, and it swung open. She tumbled out and pulled Barry with her. Once outside the vehicle she began to run and Barry trailed after her, neither of them looking back.

Andi saw them flee and soon realized she needed to escape too. She pulled the door handle, but nothing happened. She shook her head, unable, or perhaps unwilling, to believe it. She pulled the handle again, this time harder. The door still didn't open. She remembered the beating the door had just taken and wondered if it was damaged. She looked around for the shadow of Mossback, or whoever it was, and soon found it at the rear of the vehicle. She then caught a glimpse of a small flash of light and then her heart began to pound as she realized a match had been lit. Panicked, she threw herself across the car to the driver's door and as she reached for it, she realized it was too late. The car became enveloped in a hot blanket of fire. Despite the heat and flame, Andi still yanked on the door handle. To her surprise, this time it opened, and when it did, the rear door that Dana had left open created a vacuum. Before she had any time to react, Andi was burning. She screamed in agony as the clothes melted off and to her body. Her hair was now in a blaze and as she screamed, she became aware that she was literally inhaling the fire too. Seconds later, she collapsed, half her body in the car, and half out on the ground.

It was the screaming that got Dana's attention. It wasn't the sound of a terrified girl anymore, this was different. Dana knew that Andi was burning to death. The thought of it made her sick, so much so that she fell to the ground, unable to run any further.

"Don't stop," Barry said, tears streaming down his face. "We've got to keep going. He'll get us if we don't keep going!"

He grabbed her arm and tried to pull her up.

Dana pulled away from him and began to wretch. She was physically ill and in no condition to run, even if she wanted to. Barry continued to plead with her to get up. She wanted to tell him that she wanted to get up and she wanted to flee with him. But something inside her seemed to break when she realized her friend had just suffered such an agonizing death. It was as if her whole body had just suddenly shut down on. She looked over at Barry, hoping he could see the helplessness in her eyes. What she wanted was for him to run. She wanted him to get as far away from her as possible, at this point it seemed as if she were as good as dead. It was then that she felt a looming presence behind her followed by a firm grip on her shoulder.

Chapter Eighteen

Deputy Dan Briggs was as friendly as they come. He was tall with brown hair parted just right with brown eyes to match. He'd gone out of his way to be as polite as possible to Chuck and Sara, even asking if they were okay with him coming inside when they arrived at the house.

"Of course," Chuck said, motioning for him to enter. "You can't exactly babysit us sitting outside."

Deputy Dan's face flushed red from embarrassment, and he paused before crossing the threshold. "No really, I can sit in the car and keep any eye on things out here if that's better for you guys," he said, jerking a thumb back toward his cruiser parked on the street. "I don't want to trouble you."

"No, we won't have you sitting outside," Sara said. "Come in and I'll get you some tea."

"Thanks," he said, finally feeling comfortable enough to enter. "I'm sure I won't be here long. I was just told to stay with you until the sheriff returns with your nephews."

"I still think we should be over there with him," Chuck said, pulling out a chair at the kitchen table. As he sat, he then motioned for the deputy to do the same. "But I understand the sheriff's concern when he told us what was going on."

Deputy Dan nodded as he took a seat across from Chuck. "Look, I know it's hard to sit idly by and depend on someone else." He paused and leaned forward. "I just want you to know that the sheriff is a determined man. He'll find those boys and have them back here in a jiffy. You'll see."

Sara approached from behind him and gently placed a cup of warm tea onto the table. "We trust you're all doing what you think is best under the circumstances," she said with a smile.

Deputy Dan smiled back and then picked up the tea. He took a long pull. "Oh, that's good," he muttered, eyes closed. "That really hits the spot."

"I knew you'd like it," she said. "I made it just the way my grandmother used to make it."

Deputy Dan opened his eyes and looked over at her. "Who was your grandmother?"

"Her name was Anne Ross," Sara answered. "She used to run the little convenience store at the edge of town on Grasshopper Road."

He leaned back and smiled. "Ms. Anne was your grandmother?"

Sara nodded. "The sweetest woman that ever lived."

Deputy Dan nodded. "She sure was. Man, I had no idea. Whatever happened to Mrs. Anne?"

Sara swallowed. "She passed away about six years ago."

His face suddenly turned somber. "Oh, I'm sorry to hear that. Heaven gained an angel, that's for sure."

Chuck continued to watch and listen to the back-and-forth banter between the deputy and Sara. He glanced at his watch and nervously waited. Deputy Dan continued to drink the tea and when he finished it, he actually asked for more. Sara happily refilled his cup. Several more minutes passed, and Chuck began to notice him rubbing his eyes.

"Are you alright, deputy?" he asked.

"I don't know," he answered woozily. "I just suddenly feel so darned tired."

"Oh goodness," Sara said as she reached for his cup and pulled it away. "You look exhausted. Why don't you come lie down on the couch for a minute?"

Deputy Dan rose to his feet and shakily walked toward the living room. "I think I'll do that," he muttered. "Please let me know when the sheriff arrives. He'll kill me if he sees me lying down on the job."

Chuck rushed to his side to steady him as he walked into the living room. "The sheriff will never know," he said assuredly. "You just take a break. Everything's fine."

Deputy Dan glanced over at Chuck, a dreamy look in his eyes. He opened his mouth but before he could speak, he fell forward, landing hard on the couch. Chuck shot a worried glance over at Sara.

"How much did you give him?" he asked.

"Enough to keep him knocked out for a few hours," she replied.

He nodded. "Just the way Grandma Anne made it, huh?"

"She always knew how to get us kids to go to sleep," she smirked, holding up a bottle of sleeping pills.

Chuck jogged to the bedroom and flung open the closet door. He reached to the top shelf and retrieved an old cigar box. After setting it on the bed, he flipped open the lid to reveal a revolver wrapped in cloth.

"Make sure it's loaded," Sara said, looking over his shoulder.

Chuck opened the cylinder, spun it, and then closed it. "We're good to go," he said, tucking the weapon into his pocket."

As they reached the door to exit the house, Sara grabbed his arm.

"What is it?" he asked.

She bit her lip, then said, "Are you sure we're doing the right thing? Are we overreacting?"

Chuck turned to face her, placing both hands on her shoulders. "Honey, about an hour ago the sheriff told us that Kevin Parker has had some kind of unhealthy obsession with you for the past twenty-five years—and then he dropped the bombshell on us that he escaped the asylum this morning. The day he escapes just happens to be the twenty-fifth anniversary of the killings. Do you really think all that is coincidence?"

She stared at him, unsure how to respond.

"Well, I don't," he said, answering his own question. "He's obviously going to target you."

She reluctantly nodded. "Okay, I get all that," she replied. "But how can you be so certain his first stop will be Camp Beaver Brook?"

He huffed, obviously in no mood to answer questions. "Because," he groaned. "He's a psycho that killed Joe Folsom at Camp Beaver Brook. A lot of people, myself included, believe Joe—or some version of Joe, is still out there. Kevin will want to go back to finish what he started. Those boys could become collateral damage if I don't get out there fast."

"I still don't see where this concerns me so much," she said. "If Kevin's going to finish off Joe, why should I be so worried?"

"Honey, he's not going to stop with Joe—or Mossback," he said, correcting himself. "You're the last piece of the whole damn thing. I guarantee you if someone doesn't stop him, he'll be coming for you next. That is literally the only reason I want you to go with me. I'm not leaving you here alone."

"I'm not alone," she muttered, her eyes shifting to the couch.

"Deputy Dan will be out for hours," he snapped. "You're coming with me!"

CHAPTER NINETEEN

Dana felt her body being lifted and before she knew it, she was thrown over someone's shoulder and carried briskly toward the forest. She could still see the burning police car in the parking lot to her left. Barry was running directly behind her and whoever was carrying her.

"Where are we going?" she managed to ask.

"To the other side of the lake." It was Brian's voice, and his breathing was labored. "I saw an old maintenance shed over there. Maybe we can hide there until morning."

For the most part they stuck to the shoreline and Brian somehow managed to push through the relentless onslaught of dense foliage. Everything from briars to kudzu hindered his movements but somehow, he carried onward. He wondered how much poison ivy he'd stomped through but then remembered that was the least of his problems at the moment. When he could go no further, he stopped, dropping onto his knees. Dana slid from his shoulder and collapsed onto the ground.

"We can't stop," Barry said, grabbing his brother's arm. "We've got to keep going."

"We will," Brian answered, panting. "Just give me a second. Keep an eye out. Do you see anyone following us?"

Barry looked back in the direction they'd come and squinted, desperately trying to make out any movement among the speckled places where the moonlight shone through the canopy of treetops.

"I don't see anything," he said.

"Good," Brian replied, and forced himself back onto his feet. He looked ahead of them and could just make out the darkened silhouette of the old maintenance shed. "We're almost there," he muttered, pointing. "Dana, can you walk?"

She was on her back, looking directly upward at the stars. "How can such a beautiful night turn so horrific?" she asked.

Brian looked up at the sky and then back down to her. She didn't seem herself and this wasn't the time for her to mentally check out.

"Dana, I need you to get up," he said, grabbing her hand. "We're almost to the shed. You can lie down when we get there."

Dana looked over at him, but her eyes were distant. "Andi's dead," she groaned, her eyes welling up.

"I know," he answered. "And when she died, it gave you time to get away. Don't let her death be in vain."

Dana looked away and began to sob. "I'm tired," she moaned. "I'm so tired of all this. I just want it to be over."

"It'll be over soon," he said. "I promise." He glanced over at his brother. "Barry, help me with her."

The two of them pulled her up and, with each of her arms around their necks, somehow managed to steer her the short distance to the shed. Brian eyed the door and immediately felt dismay when he realized it was padlocked shut.

"Dammit," he groaned wearily. "You've got to be kidding me."

"It's okay, it's old and rusty," Barry said, clearly trying to cheer his brother up. "We can break it!"

"Are you nuts?" Brian shot back. "If we start pounding on that thing in the dead of night everyone within a two or three mile radius will be able to hear us!"

He reached for the lock and rubbed a thumb over the rough exterior. As Barry pointed out, it was indeed rusty. The shackle was worn and Brian wondered if he could perhaps pry it loose as that would be far quieter.

He gently lowered Dana to the ground where she could lay back against the trunk of a massive oak tree. She was still distant, as if her mind had journeyed away to a time and place far happier than the real one, she was physically stuck in. He began rummaging in the pile of junk that was near the rear wall of the shed.

"Come help me," he said to Barry, motioning for him to come closer.

"What are we looking for?"

"I need a hammer, a pry bar, or maybe just a long piece of steel," Brian explained. "Something sturdy enough for me to try and pry that lock open."

"This feels like nothing but old scrap metal," Barry said as he felt around in the pile.

"Probably because that's what it is," Brian quipped. "If I had to guess, this was probably used as a welding shed at one time. Be careful not to cut your hand."

They felt bits of wire, spent welding rods, and pieces of angle iron of various lengths, but nothing that would be the right size and strength of what Brian was looking for. Barry had all but given up and turned to look back down the path to make sure no one was sneaking up on them when the toe of his shoe caught something slender and heavy on the ground, causing him to trip.

"Shoot!" he yelped, falling to his knees.

"You, okay?" Brian asked as he continued to search.

"Yeah, I guess so," Barry said wearily, rising to his feet and dusting himself off. He then reached down to see what he'd tripped on and discovered a rather large open-ended wrench. "What about this?" he asked, holding the tool up into the moonlight.

"Bingo," Brian said, immediately snatching the rusty tool from his brother. "The open end of this wrench is perfect to pry with."

He marched back to the lock with purpose, taking it in his left hand. With his right hand, he wriggled one of the jaws of the open wrench under the shackle. Brian pushed down on the wrench, bearing down on it with all his weight. He clenched his jaw hard as he pushed when suddenly the wrench slipped out and clanged against the metal side of the shed. The sound echoed loudly across the lake. Brian cursed and then stood deadly quiet, listening intently for any sound that would indicate they'd been heard.

"Keep your eyes peeled," he whispered to Barry. "There's no way that whatever is out there didn't hear that!"

Barry walked to the edge of the lake to watch and listen. After a long moment, he said, "I think it's okay."

Brian disagreed but said nothing. The reality was if the sound was heard, he had to quickly get the lock free so they could hide. There was no time to wait and see. He scooped the wrench up from the ground and continued the effort. He pried as hard as he could without dropping the wrench again, but it wouldn't budge. Just as he was seriously considering hitting the lock again–because now it didn't seem like it would make much of a difference, Barry reappeared beside him.

"Brian, come here, quick," he said anxiously, and then hurried away out of view.

Brian followed him to the front corner of the shed and watched as his brother pulled back a piece of loose siding. "We can all get in through here," he said proudly.

Brian smiled and mussed his brother's hair. "Great work," he said, relieved. "Quick, let's get Dana."

When they reached her, they were surprised to find her asleep.

"How can she sleep right now?" Barry asked, dumbfounded.

"I think she's in some kind of mental state that's pulled her mind away from everything going on," he answered. "I've heard of it, but I can't remember specifically what it's called. Regardless, we've got to see after her the best we can right now."

Barry nodded and followed his brother's lead as he pulled her up as gently as he could. She stirred, opening her eyes to look at both of them.

"What are you doing?" she mumbled.

"Taking you somewhere safe," Brian replied.

They managed to lead her through the opening and into the shed. Inside, there were no windows and no space for moonlight to enter. They were in literal pitch-black darkness.

"This would've been a good time to have one of those flashlights," Brian grumbled.

"Or the lantern," Barry agreed. "For all we know, Mossback could be sitting in here with us right now."

"Don't say that," Brian snapped. "It's not funny."

"Hey, Dana," Barry said. "Can you hear me?"

There was a long silence when she finally answered. "Yes, I can hear you."

"Do you happen to have the lighter Andi gave you earlier?" he asked. "You lit the lantern with it."

"That's right," Brian said, perking up. "Check your pockets, Dana!"

They could hear her rustling about, and then suddenly there was a spark, another spark, and then a flame. "Found it," she said softly.

Brian took the lighter from her. "Thanks," he said as he turned to survey their surroundings.

He soon found an old lantern that had a small amount of oil still in it. "Cross your fingers," he said as he attempted to light the wick.

It took a moment but thankfully the lantern did light, filling the room with a golden hue. The shed was full of old lawn equipment and tools. He spotted everything from an old lawnmower next to a welding machine, to an assortment of shovels and rakes; everything covered in a thick layer of dust. Brian also noticed an ax that he promptly picked up.

"What are you going to do with that?" Barry asked.

"Obviously it's for protection," he replied. "We're not taking any more chances. We'll stay here for the night and if that thing comes around here, I've at least got this to fight back with."

As if on cue, the sound of footsteps crunching on the gravel outside could be heard. Barry's eyes widened and Brian immediately held a finger to his mouth, a stern signal for his brother to remain quiet. He glanced over at Dana and saw her seated on the ground, her eyes closed. He couldn't tell if she was asleep, but hoped she was. Brian then reached over and dimmed the light in the lantern, hoping none of it had leaked to be visible outside. Deep down he knew this was wishful thinking and immediately he second guessed his decision to light the lantern at all.

The approaching footsteps grew closer and closer until it became apparent that whoever was outside had reached the door. Brian listened intensely as the old rusty lock was lifted as if being examined by whoever was on the other side. This was followed by the sound of the lock being yanked repeatedly until finally being released, clanging hard against the metal siding. Footsteps were heard again as the being moved away. There was a brief moment of complete silence soon followed by a loud crash into the door. It was now evident that the door was being kicked. Brian gripped the ax handle tighter and tighter each time the door was kicked. It would not hold forever. It was becoming more and more apparent what he must do. He turned to look at Barry.

"Stay here with Dana," he whispered to him. "I'm going to draw it away from here."

Barry looked up at him, his eyes full of fear.

"It's going to be fine," Brian said in the calmest tone he could muster. "Stay here. I'll come back for you as soon as it's safe."

Barry was breathing heavily now, clearly becoming more panicked. Despite this he nodded and fought back the tears that were becoming increasingly hard to stop. He hated for Brian to see him cry, even during a moment as terrifying as this. Another loud crash erupted from the door, and it was now visibly bent inward.

With the ax still in his grasp, Brian hustled toward the loose piece of siding and emerged into the night air again. Slowly, he made his way toward the front of the shed and as he reached the front corner, his heartbeat so hard in his chest he could literally hear the thumping in his ears. In his mind's eye, he envisioned himself sneaking up behind Mossback and burying the ax head into the back of his skull, thus ending the nightmare once and for all. Imagining killing someone was one thing but actually doing it would be quite another. He forced himself to think of Carl, Mark, George, Nicole and Andi. None of them deserved to die, and the person responsible surely didn't deserve to live.

Brian took a deep breath and willed himself to rush around the corner of the shed. He brought the ax up over his head as he moved, ready and committed to using it with all the lethal force he could get out of it. When he rounded the corner, it suddenly occurred to him that the crash he'd heard had stopped. Once he made it to the front door, it chilled him to find that no one was there.

Brian cursed under his breath as he now found himself in a vulnerable position. For the briefest moment, he felt that he'd gained the upper hand. He knew where his attacker was, and he'd finally felt like the hunter instead of the hunted. Now that the monster had vanished, he felt vulnerable. He stood there, his head peering in all directions with the full moon shining down over him, out in the open waiting to be attacked. He wasn't just looking; he was listening for any sound to give him any indication of where the creature had gone. When he heard and saw nothing, he felt something angry beginning to build inside him. Dana had just told him she was tired of all this, and he completely knew what she meant. Brian was tired of it too; it was time for it to end.

"Come out and face me!" he yelled, his voice echoing across the lake. There was no response.

"Come out right now, you coward!"

He held the ax in front of him with both hands, ready to use it at any moment. Just as he began to believe that Mossback was cowering away from him, he heard a rustling in the nearby woods. It was the sound of footsteps again and this time they somehow sounded heavier. Brian shot a glance in the direction of the sounds and soon noticed a large, dark figure moving toward him. Again, his heart began to race. He felt his palms begin to sweat which made him grip the ax even tighter.

"That's it," he muttered. "Come on out and let's finish this!"

The figure moved toward him, slowly and methodically. Brian was stunned and a little puzzled that the monster wasn't moving faster. This, he decided, would be something he'd use to his advantage. Brian figured the last thing the creature would expect would be for him to rush straight at him, so this was exactly what he did. He clenched his teeth and charged at the massive being that was about to bear down on him. When he reached it, he swung the ax as hard as he could, hoping it would take the monster's head off with one swipe. To his shock and amazement, the ax was stopped in midair before it could deliver the deadly blow. The creature somehow caught it, with what seemed to be little effort. The weapon was wrenched free of Brian's grasp and in a mere second, he found himself unarmed, standing in the presence of a being that he could finally plainly see in the moonlight.

It was clearly a man, or at least the remnants of a man. The eyes, though yellowed, appeared human. Its body was wet and slick and covered with some sort of muddy sludge that reflected the moon. The thing was a hulking mass of both nature and mankind. The legend was true. Mossback was indeed real, and it seemed Brian would be his next victim.

Chapter Twenty

Sara was amazed that Chuck knew where to turn to find the entrance to Camp Beaver Brook. The overgrowth around the road was so dense she'd have never spotted it. He turned the car and slowly piloted it over the old two track road.

"How on earth did you remember where to turn?" she asked as the car rocked back and forth on uneven ground.

He shrugged. "Sara, after what happened there all those years ago there's not a single time that I've passed through here without glancing at this road."

"Well, I've just always avoided the area altogether, so I don't have to be anywhere near this place," she replied. "I guess that's the difference between you and me."

"What's that supposed to mean?" he asked, giving her a curious look.

"It's like I told you earlier," she answered. "I've tried to put those events behind me–to forget about them once and for all. You seem fine reliving them."

Chuck held up a hand. "No, I have no desire to relive any of that," he shot back. "But you're right, I've been unable to forget it. It's seared near the forefront of my mind."

"And the events of tonight aren't helping me put all of this away," she replied.

He sighed and shifted in his seat. What she said was the truth, but he didn't want to acknowledge it.

"Do you smell that?" she asked as they drew closer.

"Yes, smoke," he said ominously.

As they drove under the arched sign they spotted the police cruiser, or what was left of it, smoldering in the gravel lot.

"Oh my god," Sara said. "I knew something was wrong, I just knew it."

Chuck nodded. "Right, and that's why we're here," he said. "Don't panic. Stay focused and keep your head on a swivel."

When he brought the car to a halt, the headlights became fixed on another vehicle parked ahead of the police cruiser. It was Brian's Ford Pinto, and the hood appeared to be up. Sara immediately brought a hand to her mouth.

"It's fine," Chuck said, reaching over to place a calm hand on her knee. "Actually, this is good. At least now we know for sure they're here. We're going to get out, find them, and then get the hell out of here."

"But Chuck," she said, her voice trembling. "What if they're–"

"Don't," he said, sharply cutting her off. "We're not going to entertain the idea of anything bad. Stay focused. Let's find them and get out of here."

He grabbed a flashlight and they both stepped out of the vehicle, quietly closing the doors behind them. Sara couldn't help but stare at the police cruiser. There were small flames dancing inside the charred interior, providing just enough light to illuminate the ground beside the car. It was there that Sara spotted something that made her gasp and stop dead in her tracks.

"What's wrong?" Chuck asked, noticing that something had spooked her.

She opened her mouth to speak, but no words came out. Instead she stretched out her arm and pointed. Chuck moved closer to the car and directed the beam of his light toward the area where Sara was pointing. At first, he couldn't tell what exactly he was looking at, but then it hit him. It was the necklace around her neck that gave it away; it glistened when the light hit it. The burned body of a girl lay strewn between the ground and the interior of the vehicle. The corpse was burned so badly that they were unable to make out a single distinguishing feature. There was no hair left on the head, and the skin had been charred to the point that part of the skull was exposed.

"Dear god," Chuck said, his voice barely above a whisper.

He suddenly felt the overwhelming urge to flee, to just run back to the car and drive away as fast as he could. Clearly they needed help. If this girl had died so horrifically, and in such close proximity to the police cruiser, then it wasn't a stretch to assume Sheriff Turner was probably dead as well.

Chuck shook the thought from his head. Stop assuming things, he thought. Get your head right. He looked over at Sara. "Stay close to me," he muttered.

She did and they moved closer to the center of the campground. The place was, for the most part, the way they remembered it. One major difference was the trees. What had once been an open, wide space now seemed crowded by nature.

"Where should we look first?" she asked, eyeing the cabins and the dining hall.

"The dining hall is where everything reached a climax the last time we were here," he answered somberly. "I think it makes sense for us to check in there first."

She reluctantly nodded. "Alright," she said. "Let's get this over with." She took a step toward the front door when Chuck grabbed her arm.

"Not the front," he said. "We'll go in through the back."

She nodded again and then followed him around the side of the building. It was eerily quiet. When they reached the rear of the building, Chuck put his body against the wall and carefully peered around the corner.

"Do you see anything?"

He looked back at her, a bit bewildered. "I'm not sure," he whispered. "It looks like someone is maybe lying on the ground. I can't tell with all the shadows back here."

"What do we do?"

Chuck bit his lip and took a deep breath. "Stay here for a second," he said, stepping around the corner.

He felt her grab the tail of his shirt, but he pulled away. With the beam of light leading his eyes it became easily apparent that what he was looking at was indeed a body. It was the tennis shoes he noticed first, followed by the jeans, blue tank top, and then–

"Oh my god," he said, almost in a gasp.

"What is it?" Sara asked, still staying out of view.

"It's another dead body," Chuck answered. "A teenage boy."

"Are you sure he's dead?" she asked, increasing fear hanging on every syllable.

Chuck held the light on the bloody stump, all that remained of the boy's neck. He saw no sign of the head and was just fine with that. He'd seen enough gore already. "I'm a hundred percent certain," he answered Sara. He moved the light away so the grisly part of the body would be hidden again in shadow. "Okay, come on out now," he said to her as he began to approach the back door.

When he reached it, he found it partially open. His mind raced as he could only imagine everything that had possibly transpired there in the past few hours. Slowly, he reached out to push the door open the rest of the way, listening closely for any sound that would indicate someone was waiting on the other side of it. As he took a step forward, something else suddenly occurred to him. He paused and looked to his right.

"Sara?" he called out in a high whisper. "Are you coming?"

He waited and listened. There was no response, and a cold chill ran up his spine. Instinctively, he reached for his belt and pulled out the revolver as he made his way back to where he'd left her. When he rounded the corner, the shining light ahead of him illuminated a startling sight. Sara was standing in front of him, her face now white with unbridled fear. Her eyes were wide and she visibly trembled. Behind her was another figure, a large man that held a large kitchen knife pressed tightly against Sara's neck. Chuck immediately recognized the man dressed in a dark jogging suit. He'd expected to find him here. Despite the dark color of the clothing, Chuck could visibly see that he was covered in blood. The man's hands were literally caked with blood, and there were even splatters all over his face.

"Kevin Parker," he said gently. "The sheriff alerted us that you'd broken out just a little while ago."

Kevin snorted and cocked his head slightly. "The sheriff is dead," he said. "I killed him."

Sara closed her eyes when she heard the declaration and choked back the urge to cry. Chuck swallowed and tried to control his breathing. He kept the revolver pointed at them, knowing full well he couldn't pull the trigger with Sara in the way.

"Who else have you killed tonight?" he asked, not sure if he really wanted to hear the answer.

"A bunch of damned kids," he answered through clenched teeth. "I didn't come here for them, though. They just got in the way."

Chuck felt his knees get weak. He was unsure how to respond. He eyed Sara and to his surprise he noticed a change in her demeanor. Kevin's confession seemed to spark something in her that was entirely the opposite of fear.

"Kevin, I need you to let go of her," he said.

Kevin shook his head immediately. "No," he said. "Sara was the next person I wanted to find tonight."

"Why? What do you want with her?"

There was a hint of a smile. "She has to die. I'm sorry, but I missed her the first time and I've been waiting for this opportunity ever since."

Sara glared at Chuck, obvious fury beginning to build behind her eyes. "Then do it," she snarled.

"No!" Chuck yelled. "Please, don't do that. No one else needs to die!"

"I'm sorry Chuck," he replied with icy calmness. "I have nothing against you. You didn't laugh at me that day. The only people I desire to kill are Sara–and of course Joe."

"Joe is already dead you psychotic piece of sh–"

"Sara, stop it!" Chuck snapped. "Don't antagonize him!"

"You both know that Joe is not fully dead," Kevin said, seemingly ignoring Sara's insults.

"People can't be partially dead," Chuck replied. "They're either dead or they're not. And if you're referring to the legend surrounding Mossback...that's just a story to keep people away from here, Kevin!" he added, knowing full well he'd always personally believed in the legend. In the desperate situation he now found himself in, he'd say anything he could to get the upper hand.

"The only monster in this story is you," Sara spat. "Now if you're going to kill me, get on with it! If you don't, I promise you I'm going to kill you."

"And how do you plan to do that?" Kevin hissed, pressing the knife blade tighter against her throat.

"Let me go and I'll show you," she answered. "You killed my nephews and now the only thing that will stop me from killing you is my own death. So again, if you're going to do it you better get on with it!"

"You use that knife on her and I will shoot you dead," Chuck said, now feeling more desperate. "Then Joe will continue to live on and there's not a damn thing you can do about it."

Kevin breathed heavily as the possibility of being killed without the opportunity to finish Joe off seemed to strike a chord.

"I don't need the knife to kill her," he answered, casually dropping it to the ground. "I've used my bare hands all night long."

For a moment, he looked away and seemed to peer at his surroundings. "There is something about this place," he said wistfully. "Something magical, I think."

Chuck and Sara locked eyes again. He could see that, with the knife gone, she was on the verge of trying something. He slowly shook his head, a silent plea for her to be patient. Kevin was a mammoth of a man and absolutely looked capable of doing real damage with his bare hands as he'd suggested.

"Maybe if I die," Kevin continued. "Then I can come back too...just like Joe." He turned his attention back to Chuck, with a somber expression on his face. "I'm truly sorry," he said. "But this is how it has to be."

Chuck looked on in horror as Kevin brought one of his large hands to Sara's throat. She immediately caught it with both of her hands and pushed back with all the strength she could muster. The effort was useless. Kevin easily wrapped his fingers around her throat and began to dig in. Chuck had no clear shot, so he immediately shoved the gun back into his waist band and ran toward them in a panic. When he was almost there, he was met by a vicious backhanded blow from Kevin's free arm that sent him flailing. When he hit the ground, he looked up, but his vision was blurred. He could hear Sara gasping as she clawed at the hands on her neck.

"Stop struggling," Kevin muttered coldly. "It'll all be over soon when I rip your throat out."

"No!" Chuck screamed. "Let her go!" He reached for the gun again and pointed it at them, but still he was unable to pull the trigger. He simply could not make out what he was aiming for.

Suddenly, he realized that he could no longer hear Sara's gasping for air, and he feared she was dead. With no other options, he clumsily regained his footing and again charged at Kevin. He was met yet again with resistance, but this time it was different. Someone else had grabbed him.

Chapter Twenty-One

"Let me go!" Chuck growled, pulling himself forward in hopes of still being able to save Sara's life.

"Uncle Chuck, wait!" a familiar voice replied.

Chuck stopped himself and looked back to find that it was Brian holding him back. The sight of his nephew overwhelmed him with a flood of conflicting emotions. He was thankful to see that he was alive, of course, but why was he hindering him from helping Sara?

"Let me go, Brian," he yelled. "I've got to help Sara!"

"She's getting help!" Brian replied triumphantly. "Look!"

Chuck did look, and just as his vision returned to normal. What he saw relieved, horrified and astounded him all at once. Sara had mercifully been released and he could see she was on the ground, clutching her throat and breathing again. He moved his gaze upward and discovered that she was lying at the feet of a creature that he'd always believed to be real.

"Mossback," he said in amazement.

"Yes," Brian said. "And he's on our side."

Mossback was slightly larger than Kevin. He seemed to lack any clothing but was covered in what appeared to be mud and pond scum, just as had always been described by people that had claimed to see him. His eyes were yellow, but very human-like, and his mouth was curved slightly into a snarl as he glared menacingly at Kevin.

"You!" Kevin said, staring hard back at the creature. If he was fearful of him, his expression and tone did not show it. "I've been waiting a long time for this. Now things will be as they should have been. I'll finish what I started with you first, and then she's next," he said, pointing down at Sara.

Mossback did not respond with words. He instead stepped over Sara and charged toward Kevin, drawing a fist back as he did so. He threw his arm forward, narrowly missing Kevin. Instead, his fist crashed into the wooden siding of the dining hall. Splintered wood erupted from the blow and Chuck could only imagine what it could've done to Kevin's head. Kevin, still undeterred, came back at Mossback with a kick to his stomach. The blow had little to no effect. Mossback stood tall and gave Kevin a long stare that spoke volumes. Kevin, blinded by his fury and bloodthirst, quickly dove for the knife he'd dropped minutes earlier. With the knife now in his grasp, he raised it high in the air and then came at Mossback yet again, this time with the full intention of plunging the blade deeply through the creature's heart.

Mossback easily caught Kevin's arm as it swung downward. He wrenched the knife free and then twisted his arm completely around. The sickening sound of snapping tendons and breaking bone was quickly drowned out by the wail of pain that erupted from deep within Kevin's body. Mossback ignored his cries and promptly broke Kevin's neck, immediately silencing him forever. The hulking man dropped to the ground with a thud.

Mossback's shoulders rose and fell as he stared down at the lifeless mass in front of him. Eventually, he raised his head slightly, briefly locking eyes with both Chuck and Sara, before turning away to lumber back into the forest.

"No, wait," Sara called after him.

Mossback stopped, but he did not turn to look back at her. She started to walk toward him, but Chuck caught her by the arm and shook his head. She wrenched free and drew closer anyway.

"I need to know," she said. "Are you Joseph Folsom?"

The creature grunted and began to walk again. Sara crossed her arms and swallowed, her mind racing quickly as she realized her time to get answers was almost up.

"Please!" she shouted. "You just saved me, Chuck and our nephews. I want to know who to thank!"

"I'm Mossback," the creature answered in a dark guttural tone. "Now leave me be."

The words hung in the air as he began to walk again. This time there was no attempt by Sara or anyone else to stop him. She'd gotten her answer, just as Chuck had. The voice was deeper, but unmistakably familiar. Somewhere under the mud and muck, Joseph Folsom was there. He still lived.

Sara stood where she was and watched, unblinking, until he disappeared into the veil of shadowed forest. When he was gone, she turned to look back at Chuck who now approached. There were tears streaming down her face when she fell into his open arms.

"It was him," she said, sobbing. "What happened to him?"

"I don't know," Chuck replied, holding her tightly. "But he saved our lives just in the nick of time. Whatever he is now, I'm glad he was here."

Sara peered over Chuck's shoulder and caught a glimpse of Brian, standing behind them, respectfully allowing them to have their moment. "Oh, Brian," she cried out, breaking free from Chuck. She opened her arms and embraced him. "Thank god you're okay!"

She pulled back to look at him. He was wet, filthy and had obviously had quite a night. "Where is your brother?" she asked hopefully.

Brian smiled, to immediately ease her concern. "He's fine," he said. "I left him with Dana Berkley in a storage shed on the other side of the lake. That's where Mossback found me. When I realized he wasn't there to hurt me, I begged him to go and stop whoever...," he paused, looking down at Kevin's lifeless body. "Whoever that is."

"Is there anyone else?" Chuck asked.

Brian shook his head slowly, a grim expression etched on his face. It was obvious that there were indeed others, but no one else that was alive.

Chuck nodded. "It's alright," he muttered. "You're all safe now. Let's go get Barry and Dana and get out of here."

When they left the camp, Chuck drove straight to the police station in downtown Darkwood. Dana was thankful to be rescued but still almost completely silent and unwilling to speak. Barry, on the other hand, would not stop talking. He excitedly told them everything he'd witnessed and heard. Brian was glad that his little brother was so willing to talk, because he, like Dana, was not. The night had been the most traumatic experience of his life. What he really wanted to do was stop and sleep for the next two days. He watched his Aunt Sara's face as Barry talked and could see the terror building behind her eyes with each gory detail that was revealed. Uncle Chuck went on to explain that Sheriff Turner had told them about Kevin Parker's escape from the asylum, and his ongoing obsession with both Mossback and Sara–and how they knew to check Camp Beaver Brook when they discovered the boys had never gone to see *Jaws 3-D*. This brought a moment of shame that Brian couldn't hide.

"That matter is something we'll discuss later," Chuck said, making it abundantly known that there would be eventual repercussions for his disobedience.

They pulled into the parking spot near the front door and each of them filed into the police station. There was only one officer inside and he seemed both alarmed and surprised when they entered the building.

Everyone sat down on the chairs that were aligned along the outside wall, except for Chuck who immediately began to explain everything that had happened–including the death of Sheriff Turner. This news prompted the officer to curse loudly as he was clearly in disbelief. Brian glanced at the clock on the wall and realized it was almost five o'clock in the morning. So much death and destruction had occurred in such a relatively short amount of time. As he listened to his uncle, he couldn't help but notice how carefully he recreated the story surrounding the arrival of Mossback and his quick dispatch of Kevin Parker. In the version of events he told the officer, there was no Mossback. There was only him and Sara. It was they that miraculously fought off Kevin and ultimately killed him in self-defense. The officer jotted everything down as quickly as he could write and soon, he was on the phone calling the asylum relaying everything he'd learned. He also made calls to request state police and medical personnel to meet him at the campground.

A call was also made via the radio requesting assistance from Deputy Dan Briggs, but there was no response. Chuck and Sara glanced at each other, then reluctantly made it known that the last time they'd seen Deputy Dan, he'd been asleep on their couch–and it wasn't entirely his fault. This made the officer curse again and pound the table with his fist. Chuck told the officer he'd go home and check on Deputy Dan immediately and obviously fill him in on what was going on. The officer agreed but also insisted they all go by the local hospital afterward to get checked out. He assured them he'd be by the hospital later to look for them and there would most likely be more questioning.

When they arrived home, Deputy Dan Briggs had just begun to stir. Chuck helped him to his feet while Sara made coffee. Briggs began to apologize for falling asleep and began to fumble his words as he desperately searched for an explanation. Sara soon shoved a mug of steaming coffee into his hand and then matter-of-factly explained that she'd purposely given him something to help him rest earlier that night. Deputy Dan looked at her, clearly perplexed by the revelation. His gaze then shifted to the coffee he was holding.

"Oh, don't worry," she said assuringly. "This one is fine."

Deputy Dan shook his head. "I think I'll pass," he said, handing the mug back to her. "Are you saying you drugged me earlier?"

"We'll settle this later," Chuck said, rather uncomfortably. "In the meantime, you're needed at the station. It's a bit of an emergency."

Deputy Dan peered at both of them, his features no longer as friendly as they'd once been. "You're right," he said. "We'll settle this later. I truly hope you've got a good story to make me understand why you'd–"

"We do," Chuck interrupted. "I assure you, we do. But you should probably get going now."

The deputy sighed, shook his head once more, and then exited the house. No one said a word until they heard his car start and then motor away.

"Why did you tell him that?" Chuck asked, bewildered.

Sara put her hands on her hips and looked out the window as she thought. "Because he's about to find out that Sheriff Turner is dead," she said, turning her gaze back toward him. "I don't want him finding a way to blame himself for that."

"There could be some serious repercussions we'll have to deal with," Chuck replied.

"Oh please," she scoffed. "They're going to be so wrapped up in this mess, what we did to him will be a low priority for a while. By the time they ask us about it again, we'll be ready."

Chuck walked over to her and put a hand on her shoulder. "You always think you've got everything figured out."

Her eyes widened slightly. "No, I usually *do* have things figured out. Call it women's intuition. For example, I sensed the boys were in danger right away earlier tonight. I tried to tell you and the sheriff that, but all I got was repeated pleas to 'calm down'."

Chuck nodded, knowing better than to argue the matter any further–and perhaps he didn't want to admit she was right.

Chapter Twenty-Two

By the time they reached the hospital, the sun had begun to rise. Brian didn't remember much after walking through the front door. He was immediately ushered into an examination room and told to lie down. A pretty nurse walked in, handed him a tiny cup that contained a small pill, and another larger cup of water. She asked him to take it, explaining that it would help him relax. If she said anything beyond that, none of it registered due to the sheer exhaustion that had completely overtaken him. Brian quickly took the pill and soon after his eyes closed, and he drifted off into a deep sleep.

***

"Brian, wake up sweetie."

His eyes fluttered open and Sara slowly came into focus. There was an orange light behind her, and then he saw Chuck standing over her shoulder. Brian immediately wondered how long he'd been asleep. It felt as if his slumber had been nothing more than a blink of his eyes.

"How are you feeling?" Chuck asked.

Brian rubbed his eyes and gingerly sat up. After staring at both of them for a beat, he said, "I hope this is the part where you tell me everything that happened was just a bad dream."

They glanced at each other, seemingly also wishing they could tell him that.

"How long have I been out?"

Chuck looked at his watch. "Almost nine hours," he said. "They gave you something to help you rest while they looked you over."

Brian was taken aback to hear he'd been asleep for so long, and then suddenly noticed he was in a hospital gown and was clean. "Wait, what all did they do to me while I was out?"

Sara chuckled. "They took care of you, and I'm pleased to say they found no major injuries to you, Barry, or Dana."

"Where is Dana?" he asked, perking up at the mention of her name.

"With her parents now," Chuck answered. "They left about an hour ago. All three of you have a referral to see a child psychologist, but I think Dana needs it the most. That poor girl was severely traumatized."

"Uncle Chuck, I noticed at the police station last night you never mentioned Mossback," Brian said, obvious curiosity framing his words. "Why didn't you mention him?"

Chuck looked at Sara as if he were looking to her for a good answer. When she didn't offer one, he said, "Do you really think they'd have believed me? I told them what they needed to know and nothing more."

"Why was that guy so strong?" Brian said, his thoughts shifted to Kevin Parker. "He was able to do things with his bare hands that I didn't think was possible."

Chuck shrugged. "Brian, I don't have all the answers right now, but I can tell you that he was on all kinds of medications that they were giving him at the asylum with all kinds of side effects."

"Right," Sara chimed in. "Couple that with the built-up rage he'd been carrying all these years, it was just a recipe for disaster. He was a dangerous man, and I think he's always been that way."

"There were human skulls found in the old water tower," Brian replied. "Someone had even been living in there," he added. "We assumed it was Mossback. I completely forgot to tell you about that," he said with growing excitement. "Tell the police to—"

"We know," Chuck said, offering a reassuring squeeze to Brian's shoulder. "The police already checked out the tower. They found the skulls and believe they belonged to the counselors that were murdered there in 1958. Kevin kept them like a trophy of sorts. On his frequent escapes from the asylum, the tower was where he hid out."

Brian blinked as he considered that. "But how did police know to check the tower. Did Dana or Barry tell them?"

"Neither," Sara said, and she was smiling. "We have a little bit of good news, Brian."

"What?" he asked hopefully.

"They found a survivor," she answered.

Brian felt his heart skip a beat. "Really?" he asked excitedly. "Who?"

"Nicole Phillips," she replied. "She had a pretty nasty head injury but she's going to be okay. The police were able to question her, and she told them all about the old water tower."

Brian felt himself smile. "Thank God she's okay," he said. "I needed good news."

"If you feel up to it, we can head home now," Chuck said. "Your parents are on the way. We spoke to them on the phone earlier and filled them in on everything."

Brian shot his uncle a curious glance. "Everything?" he asked.

Chuck sighed. "Brian, I'm not going to tell you that you can't tell your parents everything that happened," he began. "But I do think we've got a tremendous responsibility to do our part to keep our knowledge of Mossback a secret. After all, he saved us."

"Right," Sara said. "And remember he didn't ask for anything that's happened to him. I think it's best for all of us to stick to the story we told the police. It was Chuck that killed Kevin, and it was all done in self-defense. Dana, Barry, and even Nicole don't know any different. I truly wish it was a burden you wouldn't have to carry."

Brian considered what he'd been told and for a moment wondered if he could truly keep it bottled up for the rest of his life. Ultimately, he knew his aunt and uncle were right. Despite being blamed for decades for the murders that occurred in 1958, Mossback emerged when he didn't have to and saved their lives. Joe Folsom had somehow become something other worldly, and his very existence now made Brian question everything he'd always believed to be true about his life and everything in it. The very least he could do was keep his secret safe. Mossback would continue to be a local legend for most of the people that lived in and around Darkwood. But for Brian, Chuck and Sara, he was much more than that. For them, he was more than a legend—he was the protector and guardian they never knew they needed. Ultimately, Brian decided that it wasn't going to be a burden for him to keep the secret; it was a debt that he would always owe for the rest of his days.

ABOUT THE AUTHOR

C.G. Mosley was born and raised in rural Mississippi where he still resides with his wife, Crystal, and their seven children. He's a movie buff and the love for movies often provides the inspiration for many of his books. When he's not writing, he also cohosts a paranormal podcast, *Ghostcasters*. If you liked Mossback '83, maybe check out some of his other titles listed below.

Island In the Mist
Monsters In the Mist
Terror In the Mist
Wood Ape
Baker County Bigfoot Chronicle
Rogue
Night Of the Scorpion
The Pirate Raiders
Jackson Nash And the Vector of Peril